LEAST of BROTHERS

A Novel

BY S. ROBERT EVANS

Published by Inicio Press
https://www.iniciopress.com/
Least of Brothers
ISBN: 978-1-9992490-6-9
             978-1-9992490-7-6

DEDICATION

To Gal, Charley, and all those faithful and wonderful dogs I have had the great pleasure of knowing.

ACKNOWLEDGEMENTS

Thanks to my publisher Linda, and especially my editor, Sara. A special thanks to my wife and children, who improved the story with their honest comments and suggestions. They also patiently assisted me in my many battles with computer technology.

CHAPTER 1

"You behave yourself," Ethan says softly to his horse while patting its neck. "We are about to find out what this story is about."

Moving so that the morning sun is at his back, Ethan studies the scene ahead. It is puzzling. The barn and corrals are in good repair, and the house appears well-kept, but there is none of the activity one expects on a ranch. And where is the livestock? After spending a few days scouting the place, Ethan has seen only the boy and the dog, no one else. Movement in front of the house catches his attention.

It is the boy and dog walking from the shadows of the front porch. That accounts for the only two occupants Ethan has seen while scouting this high meadows ranch. Entering a new place and not knowing who everyone is and where they are located always makes him uneasy.

Stepping to the front of the water trough, Jay shades his eyes from the morning sun. It doesn't help. The stranger on the horse is too far away to make out.

"Vishator coming, Kaisher." Jay nods to the dog.

Kaiser trots to Jay's side and watches with the intense focus of the shepherd breed. The dog inches forward, placing himself between Jay and the approaching horse and rider. Slowly lowering into a crouch, Kaiser prepares for danger.

Astride his mount, Ethan observes the boy and dog position themselves in front of the water trough and pump. The boy is casual, the dog deliberate. Carefully examining the open fields and surrounding forests, he detects no other movement. Ethan is baffled. It just doesn't figure that a boy and dog can be the only ones living here.

A clearing carved into the pine and aspen provides the open space where a simple cabin, barn, and a few sheds have been built. Fences creating various-sized pens extend into the meadow with gates facing the lush grass. It is a small-scale sheep operation, and from what little Ethan knows of such ranching, the layout appears well thought out.

For two days, Ethan scouted the territory and found this part of the high country a good fit for his needs. Now it is time to take care of the one potential problem: other people. There are two sheep ranches occupying the upper meadows. One is far enough away to avoid, but not this one. It is hard to determine whether it is an older boy or a younger man, but in either case, he appears unarmed. The dog, on the other hand, is in position for an attack.

"Wonder who it be, Kaisher?" Jay pats the silver and black coat of the big shepherd. "I like visha…vishators."

Kaiser's senses are on high alert, instinctively processing constant streams of information. The horse is completely under the control of the man and so is of less concern. The man appears relaxed. Kaiser detects no scent of fear or hostility. The stranger's hands, which Kaiser knows are a man's greatest weapon, hold only the reins. The dog observes nothing indicating the man is concealing something. Kaiser also notices that while the man keeps his face toward the boy, he often glances toward the house and barn. The stranger acts with careful confidence, something any dog must be respectful of. Kaiser's muscles coil for sudden action. It is his duty to protect the boy.

The whole scene continues to puzzle Ethan. Sure, the place is well laid out to function as a ranch and for defense against both weather and attack, but where are the sheep?

The boy couldn't have built this place on his own. The work alone would have taken years, and everything is too well thought out. Ethan thinks of his days with the Cibecue Apache and how a raid against this homestead might have fared. If defended by a man who knows his enemy, it would have cost many lives and probably would not have been worth it. Better to be patient and catch the defender out in the pastures with an ambush from the forest. Ethan smiles at his musings. *Yes, it looks safe*, he thinks, *but it will be best to pay attention until you learn more.*

As he approaches, Ethan sees the shoulders and hind legs of the big shepherd tense up. Nodding to the boy, Ethan pulls his horse to a stop. He is a good twenty feet away but wonders if he has left enough space to shoot the dog if it decides to attack. He notices the shepherd also measuring the distance between him and the boy. The dog knows his business.

"You mind your manners with these folks," Ethan whispers to the gray gelding. The horse has the stamina of its Appaloosa ancestors but the hard-headedness of its mustang side. It is the best mount he has ever ridden, and in Ethan's line of work, that is often the difference between life and death. But the horse can be ornery and impatient, and this is not a good time for that behavior.

"My name is Ethan, and I'd like to water my horse and maybe camp back near the beaver pond."

"The shwampy place?" Jay wonders why anyone would want to do that.

"Above it, actually. Nice site with trees and water where I can rest up for a few weeks."

"I guesh sho. Why ya not wantsh to shtay in town?"

"I don't care much for towns. I like being alone."

A smile creases Ethan's face. He is telling a half-truth and giving half an answer. The real reason is that he wants to lie low and give any problems from his last job time to wither and die.

"Mind asking one of your folks to come out and talk? Hate for you to get into trouble for giving permission they might not agree with."

"It'sh all right. Kaisher and I are by ourshelvesh shinsh Pa died. My name ish Jay."

That fills in the last piece of this puzzle for Ethan. The death must have been recent because the place still looks well-kept. Although he stands about six feet tall, the young fellow appears to be about thirteen or so; it's hard to tell with these... what did Talkalai call them? "Special Ones," that is it. The dog sits up and squints at Ethan, not a threat but a warning.

"Kaiser." Ethan tips his hat to the dog. "Appropriate name for him. If I give you the reins, will you lead my horse to the water trough? Maybe then Kaiser will permit me to get down and stretch my legs."

"Shore thing, mishter! Kaisher will be glad to meet you."

Ethan isn't so sure about that.

Ambling forward, Jay fumbles with the reins Ethan tosses to him. As he gathers the leather, Jay doesn't notice the slight nudge from Ethan's knees that directs the horse forward at a walk.

"What happened to your folks?"

"Momma died when I wash real shmall, leasht that wash they tell me." Jay is conscious of every expression people make when he speaks, waiting for the telltale signs of ridicule or disgust. As his papa would say, "You might not be the brightest candle in the house, but you shine nonetheless." *This Ethan is nice, like the sisters at the mission,* Jay thinks. *Bet he won't make fun.* "Pa got shick awful bad. Got sho weak I had to carry him, and you know what?"

"Tell me, Jay."

"He wash light ash a feather. Put him in the wagon and took him to the mission where the shistersh cared for him until he died."

Dismounting carefully, Ethan keeps his hands open and away from his gun belt. This dog is good at his job; Jay's pa must have rested a bit easier knowing his son would have such a capable guardian. But what happens when the dog is no longer around? *Not your concern,* Ethan thinks to himself. *You'll be long gone and living your dream.* Ethan stretches his back and legs.

"Been riding long, mishter?"

"Not long. Remember to call me Ethan, okay, Jay?"

Ethan holds out his hand while keeping an eye on the dog. Jay eagerly shakes the offered hand. The dog remains tense but still.

"Thish meansh were friendsh, doeshn't it, Ethan?"

"I'd like to think so. Now, what about my camp?"

"Where wash it again?"

"Up the valley where the beaver dammed the creek."

"Damn beaversh!" Jay waits to see if Ethan gets his joke. It is a joke he had heard his papa tell a dozen times, and it always got a good laugh. People usually don't laugh when Jay tells a joke, leastways not at the joke.

"That's a good one, Jay," Ethan says, chuckling.

"Yesh!" Jay laughs and claps his hands. "We'll be neighborsh! Would you shtay for shupper?"

"Tell you what: I have venison back at my camp. I can fetch it back here, and we'll have a feast."

"A feasht, Kaisher! Did you hear? A real meat feasht!"

After they eat, Ethan sits on the front porch and enjoys a smoke while listening to Jay. It isn't hard to get information on any subject from the boy. Whatever he asks, Jay is eager to give an answer. It seems the boy and his dog continue to live up on the ranch under the supervision of the sisters at the mission. Jay provides them with firewood, and they set him up with enough provisions for two or three weeks. Good deal for Jay, but another complication for Ethan. Jay will not keep his new neighbor's whereabouts a secret. Even so, Ethan figures he still might have enough time to hide out while any pursuit peters out.

"When do you take your next load to the mission?"

"I jush got back." Jay scratches his head. "Hey, I got a calendar Shishter Clare gave me, and that will tell me."

Jay runs into the house and quickly returns, holding a piece of paper with the numbers one through fifteen. The first five numbers each have an 'x' scratched over them. Handing it to Ethan, Jay points to the fifteen.

"After I shcratches them all out but thish one, I got to take 'em another load."

"Does anyone ever come here to check up on you?"

"Shumtime the shishtersh or Father Josheph, but not often."

Ethan nods. Not a perfect setup, but the best he can do for now.

CHAPTER 2

The news is disturbing, but ever since Sister Clare came to the West, not a week, sometimes not even a day, has gone by without some type of a problem. To describe life on the frontier as difficult is understating the case. Forget the inconvenience of the habit, although whoever designed a uniform of tunic, scapular, and cowl had clearly never been to the Southwest Territories. Out here, every aspect of life is hard, but the church does the sisters no favors with their required wardrobe. At these times, the question "Why did you choose mission work?" resurfaces, although now it is more of an annoying whisper than the loud lament it used to be.

"What did he say his name is?"

"Ethan. Hee'sh real nice, Shishter Clare, and a good cook too. We shtuffed ourshelvesh, didn't we, Kaisher?"

Jay is as happy as she has seen him since his father fell ill. When Jay is happy, he talks. Sister Clare has no trouble getting every detail, including a fairly complete physical description of the man and his horse. A stranger has set up camp on upper Cache Creek. It is on the eastern edge of the Morgan spread, where Jay's father used to take his sheep for summer grazing. It is a strange and lonely place to camp, not suitable for any purpose but grazing livestock, unless one wanted to hide out or... what?

Where is that lazy handyman? she wonders. *Always missing when I need him!* Pickles. Sister Clare thinks it an appropriate name for such an uncouth person. The man is probably wasting another afternoon discussing some inane subject with one of the locals. Mother Superior and Father Joseph may think the one-handed loafer useful, with his knowledge of the territory and homespun wisdom, but Sister Clare finds his words tiresome and his work suspect. Well, there is no help for it: the tedious task of supervising Jay's work defaults to her.

After Jay finishes unloading the firewood, Sister Clare directs him and Kaiser to collect their payment from the supply room while she searches for Mother Joachim. The Mother Superior has her finger on the pulse of everything that happens within a hundred-mile radius of the mission. She has to, because the mission serves not only the small community of Utes living tenuously between the Navajo and Apache, but the local ranchers and their supporting settlements as well.

Physically, the mission consists of adobe buildings of various sizes, arranged in the shape of a horseshoe, covering three sides of a stone courtyard. A two-story chapel and small single-level hospital stand on one side; across the courtyard is a long building with open stalls that function as stables, storage, and workshops, depending on the need. It is from one of these stalls, presently used to store the firewood Jay provides, that Sister Clare marches directly to the convent and offices occupying the back building.

As Sister Clare scans the empty courtyard and surrounding buildings, she again finds it remarkable how physically defenseless the mission is. The front wall, all of four feet in height, will be useless in stopping an attack. Considering its influence on the surrounding area, the mission truly depends on its neighbors' goodwill. Her initial feeling of vulnerability upon arriving here three years ago has been replaced with empowerment. Sister Clare quickly learned the great respect the local tribes and settlers have for the sisters. No ramparts are needed to protect this place.

Working at her desk, Mother Joachim hears the firm cadence of footsteps and immediately knows Sister Clare is approaching with yet another new problem. Why cannot the girl be calm and easygoing like the other four sisters? Strong willed and committed, Sister Clare is a force that finds no challenge too daunting to confront. It takes a great deal of persuasion—usually friendly, but sometimes with the bite of punishment behind it—to get Sister Clare to temper her approach and appreciate the value of tact and diplomacy over her preferred method of frontal assault. The girl possesses the makings of a future Mother Superior but needs much more time to learn how to lead without confrontation. She reminds Mother Joachim of another young woman she knew from years past: herself. Perhaps that is why Sister Clare is assigned here, entrusted to someone who understands her, and knows how to mentor her.

"Mother Joachim, we have a problem."

"Why, of course we do." Mother Joachim continues to write without looking up. "Please come in, Sister Clare."

Stopping in front of the desk, Sister Clare clears her throat. The younger nun hates being admonished, especially when it is done with the calm assurance Mother Joachim always manages. Nevertheless, she has breached protocol and now must decide whether or not to apologize. Sister Clare takes a deep breath and shoves her pride aside.

"I am sorry, Mother. The problem does not warrant my bursting in without announcing myself and asking permission."

"Accepted." Mother Joachim sets down her pen and leans back in her chair. "I take it this has to do with Jay Morgan."

"There is a stranger camped above the ranch."

"How do you know this?"

"Jay told me."

"And how does Jay know this?"

"Because the man rode into the ranch and asked Jay's permission."

"Did Kaiser attack the man?"

"No. From Jay's account, the man brings them food and cooks them dinner."

"Then what is the problem?"

"Why would anyone camp in the high country unless they are in hiding? Normally, a stranger would have passed through town or come in for supplies. And why would the man befriend Jay?"

"There are many reasons to befriend Jay. For one thing, the man might be a nice person."

"This is no time for humor. Jay describes a man who is on the outlaw trail."

"I am not making light, Sister Clare, but pointing out we should not come to conclusions before examining all of the facts."

"And one of the facts is that Rufe Harris wants that land."

"The man is a paper lion."

"Who has bullied the entire town. He's hired one gunman; why not a second?"

"Hmm, you do bring up a good point. Like any bully, he is only as good as the fear he creates. That young man with the white hair and fancy guns Rufe hired has cowed the townspeople, yet I don't think the ranchers have been intimidated. But they are of a sturdier breed than shopkeepers."

Leaning back in her chair, the older nun pauses and considers the situation before continuing.

"Did Jay give you a physical description?"

"Black hair, sun-browned skin, and dark eyes. Just under six feet tall, lean, and armed."

"That describes half the men in the territory, including the Indians."

Taking a deep breath to control her temper, Sister Clare glares at Mother Joachim. Has the woman not seen the white-haired gunman? He is a raw nerve waiting for an errant word or look, any reason at all to pull his gun and kill. Shortly after arriving, the man demonstrated his prowess with pistols, and while she didn't know enough to judge, the townspeople had been impressed. The man is dangerous. With this gunman's shadow lurking nearby, Rufe Harris now controls the town.

"We should find out the identity of this man." Sister Clare manages to keep her voice calm.

"Yes." Mother Joachim rises from her chair and smiles at the young nun. What she has in mind might cause her superiors to gasp and consider her lacking in good judgment, but this is the West, and necessity often dictates going into harm's way. Mother Joachim long ago learned that there exists a different code of conduct in these remote lands. Sister Clare is probably safer traveling alone in the territory than walking through a city back east.

"Go pack an overnight bag, and don't forget your warm night clothes. I think it is time to check up on the ranch, and with that pretext, you can meet Jay's new friend."

CHAPTER 3

"We should end this right now. Let me ride up there, give the half-wit a couple of bullets, and bury him where no one will ever find the body. The dog, too."

Looking up from his desk chair, Rufe Harris observes the sneer and cocky tilt of the head. His son is serious. Where did the mean streak come from? The reckless confidence Rufe understands, but more and more, Junior demonstrates a violent side that is barely under control. Thank God Deborah isn't here to see it. Yes, Deborah has a strong will, but in a righteous way. She hates his ambitions, calling them ruthless and immoral. It is why she took their daughter and moved back to St. Louis and her family. Told him to keep his land and cattle and went back to her fine life of teas and church socials. She can afford to leave with her pride and ideals because her father is well off.

Deborah never understood the struggle to reach the top because she was born into wealth. *Yes, Deborah, I do want to be a cattle baron like Henry Hooker, and I will break anyone in my path.* Rufe sometimes imagines conversations with his estranged wife. *I did learn one thing from you, dear—that it is always better to try and outmaneuver your enemy before striking. Having a reputation as a tough man is tolerated, but being considered lawless makes you fair game for everyone. That is something our son does not understand.*

"I told you we will do this my way," Rufe sighs, "unless you want the Federal Marshal on your trail."

"Why would they care about the half-wit?"

"Do you think the sisters or that old padre at the mission will sit back and do nothing? They will howl for an investigation!"

"So, how long do we wait? We need that land!"

"No, Junior, right now, all we need is the hay. With the father gone, who do you think will cut it? Jay? The sisters? This year we get the right to the hayfields; next year, we will get the land."

"What makes you so sure?"

"Winter is coming on, a tough and scary time up in the high meadows. Think Jay Morgan can last? Next year the ranch will be abandoned, and that deed I've prepared will be signed."

"I can help make it real frightening up there." Junior grins and nods. "I'm going to town to do a little planning."

After the door shuts behind Junior, Rufe glances toward a brown leather chair in the corner of the room. A thin man with white hair uncrosses his legs and sits up from his slouch. Pushing back the brim of his black hat, the white-haired man glances up at Rufe.

"You sure you can control him?" the wiry man drawls.

"He'll listen." Rufe tries to sound confident.

"Next step?"

"We visit Jay Morgan again, only this time, instead of just passing through, I'll bring up the subject of all that tall grass. You know, real neighbor-like."

"Yeah," the white-haired man says as he sinks back down in his chair and pulls the brim of his hat back down. "Real neighbor-like."

CHAPTER 4

The road, if one can dignify it with that word, is bumpy and rough. When Jay turns the big Belgian onto the trail toward the high meadows, Sister Clare actually feels relief. The wagon ride along the rutted main highway that connects the mission settlements and towns has so jostled her stomach that she is sure a case of diarrhea is in store for her. That all changes as the powerful draft horse guides them through a grove of pine that gradually climbs onto the lush tall grass of the meadowlands. She breathes deeply the crisp high mountain air. It is so intoxicating that she once confessed to Mother Joachim that it reminds her of champagne, so fresh and effervescent one feels as though one can almost drink it.

"There he goesh," Jay proudly announces as Kaiser leaps from the wagon and runs ahead. "Shepherd on patrol!"

The dog scouts in a hundred-foot arc before them, his silver and black form running on long legs that leap over and weave around the natural obstacles. Kaiser's nose, eyes, and ears are alert, evaluating every scent, every sight, every sound. A quick stop, an intense search, perhaps a taste of the grass or a clawing of earth, and then forward again.

Sister Clare seldom tires of watching the dog work. There are times she catches the dog staring at her and is sure the animal is *thinking*, that Kaiser is engaged in reasoning, evaluating. Mother Joachim dismisses such thoughts, and young

Father Campos is so scared of her questions that he excuses himself whenever she comes near. The old Franciscan, Father Joseph, has told her that certain saints, especially some of the mystics, agree with her that some animals possess special privileges. In the middle of these musings, she misses Kaiser dropping into a low crouch, circling a stand of trees, and then sprinting into the forest.

"Hee'sh caught shomtin' for shore!" Jay crows.

"What?" Sister Clare shakes her head and tries to find the dog.

"Shometing'sh in thoshe woodsh for shore. Kaisher will get it."

"Shouldn't we stop?"

"Papa shaid never shtop, let Kaisher do what he gotta do, and you jusht get to where you be going."

Kaiser reappears and resumes his patrol.

"Shouldn't we investigate what he found in there?"

"Nope. If Kaisher thought we should shtop, he'd shtop ush."

The sister scans the tree line nervously. The dog discovered something and investigated, but no sound of another animal or man or a chase or even barking ensued. Strange, yet Jay and Kaiser appear unconcerned. *How on earth*, she wonders again, *does Jay survive up here alone?*

"Jay, do you ever get scared up here?"

"Nope. Maybe shometimes when it's shtormy. Mother Joachim tellsh me that an angel ish always with me, sho I don't worry."

"An angel?"

"Yesh. And she shays Kaisher can shometime shee and talk to him."

So, Sister Clare thinks, *Mother Joachim believes animals communicate with the supernatural. That will be an interesting discussion.*

"Do you think you can take me to your friend's camp before we go to the ranch?"

"Shore enough going up there now, Shishter."

"On the way, maybe you can tell me everything you know about Ethan."

"Like what about?"

"How about starting with why you like him so much?"

"Oh, boy, and why you will, too?"

"Exactly."

Jay explodes in a running dialogue. He is so excited for Sister Clare to meet Ethan, so sure they will become best friends. Knowing that Jay might not understand why people act the way they do, Sister Clare is aware that he can discern when people are genuine. Remarkably, Jay is convinced Ethan honestly likes him. Jay relates that he never knows when the man might drop by the ranch house or suddenly appear in the forest where Jay is cutting firewood, but Ethan is always friendly and often assists him. If the man is being false, it is quite an act. Mother Superior says to keep an open mind; Sister Clare finds that hard to do.

"You know, Shishter, Ethan ish jusht like my pa! Yup, he shore ish. Doggone it, I wisht I had thought of it shooner. I bet he'd like to hear that."

"Perhaps you'll have a chance to tell him later, Jay." *Like your pa?* Frank Morgan was one of the most honest, gentlest men she had ever known. This Ethan is an outlaw on the run, of that she is sure. Yet there is Jay's description, which cannot be ignored.

Listening to Jay's stories, Sister Clare develops an interesting picture of a calm and quiet man, alert to his surroundings and wary of contact with other people, except Jay. Apparently Ethan spends time entertaining Jay with stories, explaining how to use certain tools, and even describing how machines like the loom in the Morgan house work.

And Kaiser has taken to the man, letting Ethan scratch him behind the ears. This is no small feat, as the dog takes his job as Jay's guardian very seriously.

Some of what Jay says Sister Clare decides she must discount. Good Lord, the man Jay describes is nothing short of a Walter Scott hero. Ivanhoe, indeed! Sister Clare admits to herself that she is not merely curious, but anxious to meet this man. What is this outlaw really all about? *Yes, Mother Superior, the man is an outlaw.*

Pulling the Belgian to a halt, Jay jumps off the wagon and calls to Kaiser.

"Go find Ethan! Find Ethan!"

The shepherd trots up to Jay and sits in front of him.

"Hey! You obey me and find our friend." Jay stamps his foot for emphasis.

The dog cocks his head and grins at Jay.

"Maybe he doesn't understand who you mean," Sister Clare offers.

"Or maybe he's trying to tell you both to turn around," a voice from behind them comments.

Watching the nun's hands grip the wagon bench, Ethan immediately knows why the two of them are here: Jay spoke of the stranger living near him, arousing suspicion at the mission. But sending a nun to investigate is unexpected. The woman must be pretty special to come unarmed and basically alone to check out a potential danger. Ethan smiles as he observes the nun repositioning her right hand so that it is within reach of a hatchet strapped to the side of the bench. Her shoulders relax and she steadies her breathing while those nimble fingers explore the knot in the strap.

Walking his horse forward, Ethan informs her, "Relax, ma'am. You wouldn't get it loose in time."

"Hey, Ethan," Jay says, clapping his hands and laughing, "that wash really good. Where did you come from?"

"Didn't you notice Kaiser run into the woods a couple miles back?"

"Yesh. Wash you in there?"

"Kaiser said hello, but you passed by. Can you introduce me to your lady friend?"

Sister Clare glares at Ethan.

"Thish ish Shishter Clare."

"Proud to make your acquaintance, Sister Clare." Ethan removes his hat. "My name is Ethan."

"Just Ethan?"

Sister Clare's voice is calm, but Ethan knows there is steel in the question. The woman is regaining her wits after being surprised.

"All I need." Ethan wants to keep control of the conversation, so he quickly continues. "What brings you up here, Clare?" He notices the clenched jaw and knows she gets his point.

"We came to see you, *Mister* Ethan."

Ethan smiles and thinks, *Well done, ma'am.* This conversation could be amusing, but also dangerous if he is not on his guard. He doesn't want to slip up and give any information—or arouse any more suspicions—than the woman already has.

"Tell you what, then, Sister Clare, follow me to my camp. I am guessing you were hoping Jay would take you there, and you could have a good look before I was the wiser."

"That was my plan." Sister Clare returns Ethan's look with calm defiance.

"Hate to disappoint, so after I take you there, I'll step away and let you search for whatever you are looking for."

"That will be satisfactory." Sister Clare knows the man has her at a disadvantage, but she has a few tactics of her own to at least regain even ground. She decides to act as if she is being totally candid. "Although we both know the only reason you would allow such a thing is because every item that will tell me who you really are, as well as why you are here, has been removed or hidden."

"I certainly hope so, ma'am," Ethan says with a grin, "and if not, I am betting on you to find them."

The camp is well situated. Set back in the trees, with no path or other markings to give away its location, a small canvas lean-to provides shelter from the night and inclement weather. The canvas blends in with the surrounding boulders; an inattentive person could easily travel by and not notice it.

Ethan and Jay sit on a boulder watching as Sister Clare searches Ethan's belongings. She is certainly thorough and makes no apologies about prying into his personal items.

"What'sh she doin'?"

"Protecting you."

"From what?"

"Strangers who might want to harm or steal from you."

"Then why ish she looking through your shtuff?"

"She wants to make sure I am not out to harm you."

"But you wouldn't hurt me."

"She isn't sure about that."

As Jay tries to figure out why Sister Clare is so suspicious, Ethan uses the time to take the measure of his inquisitor. She wears the black and white outfit typical of the sisters he is familiar with at the Indian missions. She is younger than most, or maybe he just remembers them all being old because he had been a kid when he was first aware of them. Her skin has the olive complexion of some of the French and Italian folks he has known. Her serious eyes are at odds with the full lips that occasionally turn up at the corners in a half smile. Strands of black hair escaping the confines of her cowl stir wispily in the breeze. Not much specific about the rest of her figure, except a wiry frame moving about as agile as a wildcat. She is about five foot five, maybe an inch less without those black boots. Ethan realizes he finds her pretty and wonders if he should be embarrassed thinking about a nun that way. He shakes his head and looks away.

"You two are shupposhed to be friendsh."

"Not all friendships start out that way, Jay. As often as not, people let rumors and reputations and prejudices get in the way of how they evaluate others. Think of how some folks treat you badly, and they don't even know you."

Jay nods. He knows all too well how that feels. It makes him feel sad and bewildered all at the same time. Some folks laugh and belittle him just to be mean. *Why do people do that?* he wonders.

"Give Sister Clare some time. She's a good person, and we might yet become friends."

The first thing Sister Clare does is walk casually about the camp, making sure she gets a good look at the horse and tack. The animal is well cared for, as are the saddle and bags. No initials or other clues to help her discover the man's true identity. The horse eyes her suspiciously, and she decides to keep a safe distance. The cooking gear is well worn but about as clean as one can expect when living outdoors.

Entering the sleeping area is interesting. *Men really do smell differently,* she thinks. The odor from the bedding and the few spare clothes is not unpleasant, just strange: a combination of coffee and tobacco and campfire and sweat and horse and hay and.... She shakes her head and smiles. The definition of "musky," perhaps? There are two books next to his bedroll: a volume of Shakespeare's histories and the Bible. No name or initials or testimonials in either. There are notes written in pencil in each book, but she detects no pattern, just random thoughts that reveal one important point: Ethan is insightful and thoughtful. He is not the crude man she initially thought.

Clapping her hands together to remove the dust and dirt, the nun backs away from the lean-to and straightens her back. Sister Clare purses her lips and inhales deeply. She is trying to make up her mind about this "Ethan." She is convinced that isn't his true name. Is she missing something in there that might offer a clue? She will go over every item in her mind later when she is alone and can think better. She strides deliberately toward Ethan, halting in front of him with her hands on her hips. She cocks her head and examines the man from boots to hat.

"Find anything of interest?" Ethan asks casually.

"Yes."

The nun pauses and watches Ethan closely. He acts neither surprised nor panicked at her comment.

Ethan keeps his face unconcerned. The woman is strong and cunning. She is of the type that impresses the Apache and Navajo: calm and fearless, regardless of the situation. That levelheadedness and practical nature, so admired by the southwest nations, have allowed the sisters entry and staying power in this demanding land.

"Shakespeare and the Bible. They are well read. But, then, I suppose a man like you wouldn't carry an item unless he uses it."

"I have found books and horses to be good company. Better than most people I know." Ethan grins at the hard-eyed nun.

"And dogsh!"

"They may be best of all, Jay." Ethan tousles Jay's hair. "If you are done, ma'am, I think it best to get you back to the mission before dark."

"Thank you for the courtesy of allowing me to examine your camp," Sister Clare says as she executes a mock curtsy.

"You made the right decision not getting any closer to the horse. He can be a bit particular about who he lets get close."

"Like his owner?"

"I suppose so, ma'am." Ethan smiles sheepishly and turns slightly red.

Surprised by Ethan's blush, Sister Clare takes a deep breath. Who and what is she dealing with? This is not at all what she expected. There is a lot more to this man, and she will find it out, all of it.

"Can we escort you back to the mission?" Ethan is expecting her to decline.

"I am staying with Jay this night."

"Then I'll fix us dinner."

Before Sister Clare can protest, Jay lets out a delighted whoop and grabs her arm. He talks non-stop as he leads Sister Clare back to the wagon, describing what a grand feast awaits. The variety of meals Jay mentions, all probably swimming in grease, makes her queasy.

Jay clambers onto the wagon bench and eagerly unties the reins. Sister Clare accepts Ethan's offered hand and climbs up alongside Jay. She can tell a lot from a person's hands. The hand she holds now is strong and calloused, yet displays a dexterity and surprising gentleness. Of course, a gunfighter would need strong, nimble hands and fingers, but gentle?

"The big hoss looks good, Jay, and tells me he's ready to head for the barn," Ethan comments as he examines the Belgian.

"Oh, boy, a feasht!"

"I brought some vegetables and rosemary from the mission. I was planning to cook supper for Jay and myself," Sister Clare offers hopefully.

"I was hoping so, Sister." Ethan nods, choosing to overlook the fact she excluded him and is attempting to take over his cooking duties. "Carrots and onion are about as good as a cook can hope for. Have a couple of nice rabbits I left at Jays earlier, and I think..."

What Ethan thinks, she will never know. The man's attention is focused on the ground in front of the draft horse. She knows Ethan has seen something that portends danger. Sister Clare keeps attentively quiet while he investigates. Having spent a few years in the West, she has observed a number of trackers and scouts and feels she can distinguish between the capable and the incompetent. The mistake prone never last long, and, unfortunately, neither do those who rely on them.

Slowly mounting his horse, Ethan rides forward, casually examining their surroundings. Sister Clare knows the routine. She considers herself an expert at trying to appear complacent when deeply concerned or even frightened. From Ethan's actions, she surmises they are being watched. Could it be Rufe or his hired gunman? For the first time, she hopes the man she suspects of being an outlaw is as formidable as she fears. He might not care to protect her, but she is aware that he likes Jay enough to defend him. Ethan circles his horse back to the wagon and draws up next to Jay.

"Jay, do you remember telling me how Ba'cho sometimes visited your pa?"

"Yup."

"About how often did he visit?"

Jay blinks and drops his head. A long pause follows before Jay shrugs and shakes his head.

"Did he visit after your pa died last spring?"

"No." Jay's face brightens with relief.

"How about last winter before your pa got sick?"

"Yup! He comesh by before the winter."

"Is winter when he usually came to stay awhile?"

"Yup, we cutsh the grash and shtored it for hish horshes. Every winter we do that, and he shometimsh bringsh ush meat. Pa ashked him to eat with ush, but he never did."

Kaiser creeps on his belly through the long grass, his nose moving from earth to air, head slowly swinging back and forth, searching for the scent. The horses are easy to follow and have hint of familiarity, but Kaiser exercises the caution of his breed. It is not the horses he needs to fear but the men riding them. Their scent will identify them. Kaiser knows they are hiding in the forest, but he dares not approach much closer. It is the crunching sound of pine needles being stepped on that halts him. He has been dis-covered, or at least the men know he is nearby. He hears the footsteps of their horses. Kaiser remains still. They are all together and approaching his front. The horses stop, and a man's voice calls out softly. Kaiser sits up. He knows the voice and the man. At once he catches the scent of the man and those with him, separating the odor of those he recog-nizes from previous encounters and the new men. Kaiser waits. The man speaks again, and Kaiser remembers the man uses a different cadence and tone than Jay and his people.

"I see you now, wolf dog."

Kaiser's eyes keep a keen watch on the men. They smell of meat fat and animal skin and sweat. He senses no anger and sees no weapons, yet Kaiser plans his bolt to safety if the situation changes.

"We hear the father is dead, wolf dog. Are we still welcome?"

The speaker nods toward the wagon.

"There is a man with the boy. The man looks strong and dangerous. He is with a holy woman. You can tell me much, wolf dog."

The speaker points to the woods, and the other men back their horses into the shadows.

"Come, brother wolf, and I will find out what you know."

Back at the camp, Ethan smiles at Sister Clare, trying to put her at ease while warning her about their predicament. "It's like this, ma'am. Pony tracks from the east. They milled around in front of the wagon before heading into the cover of the trees you see just under my chin. They're sizing us up right now. About a half dozen or more."

"They must not think we present much of a threat." Sister Clare calmly returns his smile. "Only one of them is riding toward us, with Kaiser leading the way."

"Jay, if that is Ba'cho I'd like you to give him a friendly wave."

As Jay waves a greeting, Ethan casually turns his horse to face the visitor. Sister Clare notices Ethan slightly straighten his right leg, hand resting on his thigh; his revolver within easy reach. She offers a quick prayer that she will not have to find out how fast he is on the draw.

Keeping his mount at a walk gives Ba'cho time to examine the man. It also is a good lesson for his brother Carlos and the other younger men waiting in the trees to learn how to approach friends in the company of a stranger. The dark eyes and sharp features are familiar to Ba'cho, but it is the horse that identifies the man. The black bristles of the mane, gray coat, and faint spots on the rump belong to the mustang and Appaloosa mix gelding ridden by only one man. The horse is known for its speed and stamina and is as famous as its rider. It is said that three Comanche tried to steal the animal and were left dead along the trail as a warning: one man bucked from the horse's back and broke his neck, while the other two were gunned down before they could escape. Ba'cho has seen man and horse once before, from a distance. The man had been riding hard, eluding pursuers who were not his match. He is called "Apache Jack" by the white men, but to the Cibecue who raised him, he is known as "Cactus." He has ridden with the Red Canyon people, and it is said he knew Talkalai. This man is an outlaw, a hunter of men. Ba'cho knows this is a dangerous warrior, but he also knows the man has the reputation of being honorable. It is Cactus who saved the life of Naki-Chaa, and that is a familiar story around many White Mountain campfires.

White Mountain Apache, Ethan thinks. He knows their dress and horses well. The White Mountain clans don't think much of the Red Canyon people and therefore will be unimpressed that Ethan lived with the Cibecue. Jay tells him that Ba'cho and his people are good neighbors, wintering their horses around the ranch and providing Jay's pa peace and provisions in exchange for a portion of the hay. Back when the ranch was getting started, that would have been a good arrangement; it is probably why Jay's pa succeeded where others failed. This answers Ethan's question of why the Apache tolerated this place and why it has thrived.

About thirty feet from the wagon, Ba'cho halts and stares at Ethan without expression. Ethan returns the stare but allows the corners of his mouth to maintain a casual smile in response.

Observing the two men, Sister Clare thinks it remarkable how similar they are. Their lean faces, dark in every feature; their postures and manners calm, yet belying the coiled muscles ready for action. If she didn't know better, she might think they were brothers.

"Hiya, Chief," Jay shouts.

"I see you, Jay Morgan," Ba'cho responds in English without moving.

The two men stare at each other until the air becomes tense with the expectation of action. Sister Clare's emotions evolve from apprehension to frustration to anger. How do these men of the West come by their code of honor? All those boys who pretend to be King Arthur and his knights when at play must all come to the frontier so they can live out their daydreams as adults. Finally, she has enough and stands up, clapping her hands for attention.

"What kind of silly game is this? I should grab you both by the ears and drag you into the woods for a switching!"

Both men continue the stare down.

"She is spirited but impatient," Ethan comments in Apache.

"The holy woman is not Apache," Ba'cho responds in Apache. "I know of you. Are you Cactus or Jack in this place?"

"Here I am Ethan. You are early. We did not expect you until winter."

"The father is dead, and we came to see if the grass will be cut."

"It will be." Ethan immediately decides to fulfill the pledge of Jay's dead father. Actually, he considered it the moment Ba'cho rode forward from the trees. He isn't one to stick his nose in another's business; doing so usually results in nothing but trouble. For whatever reason, though, he is fond of Jay, and bringing in the hay feels like the right thing to do. Admittedly, there is another reason Ethan makes the promise, one that both surprises and concerns him: he wants to prove to Clare that he isn't the man she thinks. Ethan puts that thought to the side to sort out later.

"I will help the boy keep his father's promise." Ethan nods toward where he has left his gear. "My camp is set back in those trees. Appreciate it if your men left it alone while we work."

"I will tell Carlos. My brother is young and takes many men when one is enough."

"I saw their tracks."

"Then you have counted our number. If people hunt for you, know we have seen no sign of others. Only the local people have we seen."

"Thank you."

"Goodbye, wolf dog." The Apache nods respectfully to Kaiser as he rides away.

"Thank you for not interrupting again, Sister," Ethan says in English.

"I had no need to," Sister Clare responds in Apache.

CHAPTER 5

Ethan is not surprised. He knew there had to be a reason the nun did not insert herself into the conversation; she understood every word of it. Now there will be questions that cannot be avoided. Sister Clare will protect the boy, and if Ethan is not forthcoming with information, she will seek it elsewhere. That will eventually mean his whereabouts become known. It is too bad; Ethan likes this place. He has to admit that he also likes the people he has met here, even if there are only three of them.

They travel in silence to the ranch house. On his horse, Ethan lopes ahead of the wagon and examines the grounds. There are more horse prints, but not from Ba'cho and his White Mountain folks; these mounts are shod. Ethan takes a quick ride around the buildings. The place is undisturbed except for the hoof prints.

"Were they here?"

These are the first words Sister Clare has spoken since her Apache disclosure.

"No. The tracks are from shod horses, two that rode up here to the house and a third ridden by someone who held back by the pens. These two circled the house, and then they all gathered in front of the barn. Was earlier today, probably a few hours after sun-up."

"Shum vishatorsh, and we mished 'em? Doggonit!"

Ethan's and Sister Clare's eyes meet. Ethan is positive she knows who was here, and they weren't being neighborly. He nods that he understands.

"We can discuss this, and other matters, after supper," she avers.

"Jay and I will get the horses settled in and store the livery." Ethan smiles.

"But you are returning to your camp tonight."

"Nope. Jay and I are bunking in the barn tonight."

"A campout?" Jay claps.

"Yep."

"We will discuss all of this later," the nun says, glaring at Ethan.

"You can fuss all you want, ma'am, but that is one subject that will no longer be discussed." Ethan shrugs and dismounts.

Sister Clare removes her satchel from the wagon bed along with a burlap sack filled with vegetables.

"Ethan, you and I can bring the resht in, can't we?"

"Sure enough."

"Oh, boy, a campout!"

Gritting her teeth in aggravation, Sister Clare does admit she feels safer knowing he's around. Even if he is, as she now is certain, a gunman. Not knowing his reputation, Sister Clare wonders how good, and dangerous, he is. Ba'cho showed the man respect; that is probably as good a recommendation as she can get.

CHAPTER 6

The man knows how to cook, and it takes all of her Christian charity to break her stony silence and commend him. His use of native herbs gives a zest to the vegetables that reminds her of the southwest land she now lives in: heat and mineral and the earthy fragrance of sage. If only there were a glass of wine to accompany the meal! Sister Clare sighs at the thought of yet another sacrifice in her service as a missionary.

After supper, as Sister Clare stores the canned goods before sweeping and dusting, she spends the time observing the outlaw. Ethan's fondness for Jay is not feigned; it is natural and without any condescension. Remarkable that such a violent man can have such qualities. Taking a deep breath to clear her thoughts, Sister Clare closes her eyes. *Put everything you know in the back of your mind and take a fresh look as if seeing him for the first time.* Opening her eyes, she tries to reevaluate. First impression: Ethan is handsome, confident, and amiable, and he appears capable in whatever he takes on. He also gives the impression of being in control of each situation, and that makes him dangerously impressive to men... and women? Thinking of her own two sisters, she can believe how easily swayed a woman would be in his company. Reconsidering from this new angle, she tries to detect anything to give her reason to suspect his intentions are evil. There is nothing. No indication that he poses a danger to

Jay. What about his treatment of her? Again, every gesture and manner displays the odd courtliness of a man of the West, not a hardened outlaw. Yet even the White Mountain chief knows he is a gunman and on the run. However, Ba'cho also treats him with respect. Why would a man like Ethan do anything that is without personal benefit?

"If you don't mind, ma'am, Jay and I will check on the horses. When I get back, we can have that talk."

Sister Clare nods and follows them to the door. The western sky fades from pale to navy blue, covering all the shades between. She attempts to count the stars as they appear, remembering which is first and second and third. Well, that one is Venus, the evening star. She hears her mother's voice reminding her to make a wish on it. Taking a deep breath, she smiles. *Just like when you were a girl experiencing the joyous end of a summer day.* Sister Clare shakes out her wool shawl and wraps it around her shoulders. What should she wish for?

Bringing an oak rocker onto the front porch, Sister Clare sits. Stretching out her legs sets the chair in motion. Once more she gazes into the heavens and allows the universe to guide her thoughts back to youth and play and the summer warmth that wraps itself around a child like a grandmother's loving hug. What happened to that little girl? *Mother and father had the store to run, and your two older sisters were always too busy with their boys and socials and, well, it fell to you to be the studious one. Is that how it happened, or was there always something more to life that you discovered and they had overlooked? You always loved school, but it was the teaching more than the learning that attracted you. Is that what set you on this path? The journey to serve that led you to St. Anthony's Mission and Mother Joachim and Jay Morgan and this strange man?*

"You can get lost in a sky like that."

"Hmmm," Sister Clare pleasantly agrees until she remembers where she is and who is speaking to her. Glancing at

Ethan and discovering he too is gazing skyward, she once again relaxes. "When I was a girl, my father taught me about some of the constellations. I would think about the Greeks who named them and the mythology they are based on. I read how Paschal contemplated the universe until it over-awed him, and he feared it was too great to comprehend."

"Sounds like a smart man. Some things are meant to stay a mystery."

"Like you, Ethan?"

"Didn't mean it quite like that, ma'am," Ethan says with a chuckle, "and I don't think you will let me off that easy."

Sister Clare smiles at Ethan and shakes her head. *Not a chance of that*, she silently agrees.

"If you don't mind my asking, Sister, how did you end up here? I mean, being a nun out here in Apache country."

"I suppose since I am expecting full disclosure from you, it is fair to answer your question." Sister Clare is surprised how easy it is to converse with Ethan. There it is again, his ability to take charge of a situation. She must be more on guard about that. "Perhaps it will inspire you to be more forthcoming." She smiles sweetly at him and thinks it a good response.

"Meant no offense, just curious." Ethan shrugs, smiles shyly, and lowers his eyes.

Sister Clare's expression turns rueful. He has disarmed her again. Ethan is either a consummate actor or genuinely straightforward and honest. She decides to go forward with her tale.

"My father and mother own a store in St. Louis, dry goods mostly. They are wonderful parents, and my sisters and I had a blessed childhood. Michelle, my oldest sister, helps run the store with her husband now. My other sister, Marie, married a young Army officer and lives in San Fran-cisco. Both of them always loved the balls and parties and social gatherings, but at a young age I chose to help mother every Sunday at an orphanage. It was there I discovered that many children did not have parents who could care for them, who would hug them, who wanted to share in their hopes and dreams. I want to provide some love and care for those who are not as fortunate as I have been. So I dedicated my life to serving others."

"Not an easy life, Sister."

"But a very rewarding one, Ethan. Even if no one ever says 'thank you,' I know God is saying it to me."

"That enough for you?"

"Yes, Ethan, it is. How about you?"

"I'm probably one of those children you set out to help. My folks were ranchers until they were killed in a Comanche raid." Ethan's voice is matter of fact. "An uncle took me in and, after he almost beat me to death while he was drunk, I took off. An old Apache Army scout caught me trying to steal a loaf of bread and decided I wasn't as bad a case as the baker thought I was. He became a mentor of sorts, and we later moved back to his people. That was where I would roam about the desert with the one thing I still had from my dad: his Army Colt. I'd practice all day and explore the sky at night. That was where the name 'Cactus' came from. They thought I looked just like the cactus I wandered around in."

"Are you sure it isn't the prickliness of your nature?"

Ethan smiles and continues to gaze skyward. He removes a paper and tobacco pouch and rolls a cigarette.

"Sister, I will answer any question you ask of me, but I want two things in return."

"I won't—"

"Just listen before getting all obstinate."

There is something earnest in voice and manner that causes her to snap her mouth shut and nod.

"First, call me Ethan, especially in front of the boy. He won't understand any other names I might go by. Second, until we get the hay in, please do not go around asking questions or telling anyone I am camped up here. Afterward, I don't care what you say and do, but be careful how you speak around Jay. I really am the friend he thinks I am. You see, I also know what it's like to be alone and different."

It is unexpected and sounds sincere, but she considers it might be a trap to gain her silent complicity in whatever scheme he may in reality be planning. Her main concern must be for Jay; he is the mission's responsibility now. The ranch is valuable and already attracts the attention of people who believe it will be easy to take from Jay. She must remember that this Ethan is an outlaw and should not be trusted, no matter how sincere he seems.

"I will not make that second promise."

"Then I will pull up stakes and leave tomorrow."

"What about your promise to Jay and Ba'cho?"

"If they can trust me, why can't you? You are in the forgiving business; they aren't."

Ethan exhales a long stream of smoke and steps from the porch.

"Please wait a moment." Sister Clare's initial response to his request has been reflexive, and she regrets it. Besides, he is right. She has been too quick to judge. Considering the man and his early life, she is curious to know more about him. She resumes her rocking.

"Why did you agree to bring in the hay?"

Ethan pauses and decides to hedge on the truth. He begins with a reason he knows she will believe before giving her the real one.

"I'd like another two weeks before heading out. I also figure if the hay is here, Ba'cho will look in on Jay after I'm gone."

"One can forgive and yet not trust, and therefore the two are quite different. I do not know enough to determine whether forgiveness is even warranted, but I do know enough at present to not totally trust you... yet."

Looking up at the stars, Ethan considers what she's said. He finally nods and turns to face her.

"Understood, ma'am. You have reason to be cautious, and I have reason to leave."

"I will go this far, Ethan." The use of the name has her desired effect: he is listening. "Answer my questions, and if I don't accept your previous terms, I promise to give you at least a one-day warning before I make any further inquiries."

"Hey, Ethan!" Jay yells from the barn door.

"I'm here, Jay."

"You wantsh me to roll out your shtuff?"

"That'd be fine."

"Oh, boy, Kaisher! A campout!"

Ethan is giving her the stare of a wolf. She hopes her face appears calm because she is suddenly cold with the apprehension of what might happen next. Thank God she is not a man! Holding her rosary beads, she wonders if this is what one of his victims feels like before the draw. Ethan nods.

"Okay, then, ma'am. Not for you, but for the boy."

Trying not to let out the huge sigh of relief her body demands, Sister Clare composes herself as best she can while keeping hold of the beads and sending up a silent prayer of thanks.

"How do you make a living, Ethan?"

Throwing the butt of his smoke into the dirt and stepping on it, Ethan smiles. He sits on the porch and leans back on his elbows.

"Well, Sister Clare," he says, grinning at her, stretching out his legs, and crossing them at the ankles, "I see you are a direct woman. I settle disputes."

"So does a judge."

"Not out here, at least not yet. It's like this: a man comes to me and has a problem with his neighbor over water rights.

Seems all is well until the neighbor hires men to keep the man's cattle from drinking. He gets desperate, and the law is too few and too far to help. I am brought in and try to reason with the neighbor and, if need be, show him why it's better to be cooperative. Sometimes it all works out friendly like; often as not, only one side is left standing. I don't start the gun play, never have."

"So, you have some moral code to justify your profession?"

"You should maybe withhold judgment until you know the whole tale, ma'am."

Regretting her sarcastic tone, Sister Clare asks Ethan to continue.

"I already mentioned learning how to use my pistol in the desert. Well, my mentor, he saw I had the talent to do a lot more. Gave me a Winchester and taught me how to use that too. Wasn't satisfied 'til he thought I was as good as any man he'd seen with either weapon. Knew a bit, he did. Great tracker and a top hand with horses. Made sure I was proficient at those, too. Once we finished that schooling he broadened my education a bit, you might say."

Ethan gazes into the night sky, picturing the past against the blackness. Sister Clare wants to break into the silence, but instead she sniffs loud enough for him to notice, hoping it will prompt him to continue. Ethan smiles but Sister Clare isn't sure if it is at the sound or a memory. After a moment, Ethan takes a breath and continues.

"Well, one of the things he has learned in life was how to grow things, especially fruit trees. He could take an apple tree and graft on little branches from other apple trees and produce three and four different types of apples from the same rootstock. The man has a knack for growing trees. Whether smelling the blossoms in spring or eating the fruit in the fall, I loved that place. It was a small place, but it was everything I could imagine a home should be."

Sister Clare watches, fascinated, as the outlaw stares into the heavens. In the delicate light of the night lantern, she sees the enchanted face of a young boy. She surmises Ethan is dreaming, describing a place and time with hope that it might come true. Not something from the past, but a future place and time he dares to believe he will actually see.

Ethan realizes he has been caught disclosing his private musings. After a quick, embarrassed glance at Sister Clare, Ethan clears his throat and continues with his narrative.

"It seems a rancher didn't like how my friend was using the water for the trees. This rancher had some of his hands set an ambush and left Naki-Chaa for dead. Lost some use of an arm and eye and limps a bit, but the ornery old scout survived." Ethan's eyes narrow and his jaw clenches. "Every last man was hunted down and brought to justice."

"You killed them all?"

"I had help. Afterward I sort of drifted a bit until I was hired on at a cattle ranch where I discovered I was expected to rustle stock from the neighboring family outfits. I quit, and when I told the oldest son of one of the neighboring spreads what was happening, his dad hired me on. First man I caught rustling I took to the sheriff, who seemed to be real put out with my interference, and he let the rustler go. The next man I caught pulled on me, and I shot him in the shoulder. Wounded him on purpose so he would tell the others how fast I was. I wanted them to think twice before pulling on me again. They tried to ambush me, and they found out the hard way I was a better tracker than they expected a white man could be. That is where 'Apache Jack' came from. Next they hired some local gunslinger with a fearsome reputation to get me. I made sure we had witnesses when he drew on me, and afterward the big outfit became right neighborly. That's how I got started."

"How long ago?"

"About seven or eight years."

"How many have you killed?"

"I never counted. It's not like that, Sister. You want things to go easy, but.... Let's just say that I've done my share."

"And you feel quite justified?"

"Yes, ma'am, I do." Ethan looks her directly in the eyes. "I believe every man I shot, dead or not, deserved it. I will go with you and face the Maker and not feel guilty about any of it."

Stunned at first, Sister Clare considers the assertion and suddenly wishes Mother Joachim or Father Joseph were present. Ethan believes what he says. The man feels no remorse.

"But killing is wrong!" Sister Clare shakes her head as if to ward off the thoughts of justification trying to enter.

"That so?"

"Yes, that is so." Sister Clare has the feeling Ethan is a more formidable thinker than first impressions indicated. "You've read the Bible."

"I have, ma'am. Lot of killing in it. David killed Goliath, Samson killed the Philistines, and Joshua wiped out a whole city. All believed they were justified. People fight for a lot of different reasons, so let me put it plain and simple: coyote is killing your stock, and you either kill the critter or lose your ranch. Coyote is doing what's natural, he's hungry, so I'll kill him, but I also feel sorry for him. We are both just trying to survive. A man, on the other hand, often does things out of greed or just meanness. Only way to make someone like that come to their senses is let them know you'll go all the way. If they don't become neighborly, I figure they're making the choice to die, not me making the choice to kill 'em."

"Ethan, you are being paid to kill!"

"No, ma'am, I'm paid to protect a person's home. When I arrive, people know they best be reasonable and settle matters, or the consequence is risking death. Things usually get worked out. Fact is, that's why I am here. Settled a boundary dispute for Old Man Todd, and he figured he didn't owe me but half my fee because I didn't fire a shot. Took my full earnings at gunpoint, and he sent his three boys after me. Not wanting to hurt the boys, I decided to let 'em chase their tails for a while until they get tired and go home while I lay low."

Standing up and stretching, Ethan glances over at the nun. The candlelight from the lamp flickers across her profile. She gazes into the night, lost in her thoughts. Once again, Ethan is reminded of how pretty she is. Everything about her, looks and mind and even strong opinions, he finds attractive.

"Hey, Ethan." Jay trots over to them. "We gotsh to get up early, 'member?"

"Yep. We'll load up and get started after breakfast. Sister Clare." Ethan looks down at her and adds, "Let me know how we stand tomorrow."

"Yes." Sister Clare remains seated, still gazing into the night. "At breakfast."

"Tomorrow morning those three men will return. I'd like to know what to expect."

"I can handle the situation."

"A heavyset man and two hands, one a sawed-off younger fellow who bears a resemblance to the fat one, another with white hair riding a pinto. They have ridden past my camp before. They come up through the canyon trail to the east of town. They always pack for trouble, ma'am."

"Rufe Harris and his son," Sister Clare sighs. She might as well tell him and prevent him from creating a scene tomorrow. "Rufe Harris thinks he can trick or bully Jay into selling him the ranch. The white-haired man is a gunman Rufe hired. It is a situation Mother Joachim is aware of and can control."

"Who is Mother Joachim?"

"My superior."

"She good with a gun?"

"Not every dispute is resolved by the threat of bloodshed," Sister Clare says, bristling. "There are more powerful weapons than guns. We do not need your help dealing with Rufe Harris."

"All the same, ma'am, I'd appreciate it if they come calling, you stay inside."

"I will not."

"I was afraid of that. Good night, Sister Clare."

CHAPTER 7

It is hard to sleep with two pair of eyes staring at you in anticipation. Ethan tries to keep his own eyes shut and pretends to be asleep. He estimates it to be about an hour before sunrise. He expects Jay to be excited, but Kaiser? *Go to sleep, dog!* Ethan fell asleep knowing he would need a good rest with a full day of work ahead. Setting up in the meadows and getting Sister Clare back to the mission will take a while; they'll probably lose an entire day of cutting. A good night of sleep would have been welcome. Now he realizes he won't get it. The big Belgian snorts, and even Ethan's own horse joins in the general morning stir.

"Oh, I give up," Ethan grouses, opening his eyes to find Kaiser's smiling face three feet away. He swears the dog is laughing at him.

"Oh, boy!" Jay jumps up and rushes across the yard toward the house.

Brushing aside the thought of stopping the boy from waking Sister Clare creates a smile on Ethan's face. Having missed out on the campout, Sister Clare is probably looking forward to Jay interrupting her sleep, followed by an enthusiastic recounting of bunking in the barn. *Would love to see her reaction*, Ethan thinks.

Pumping a bucket full of water, Ethan washes his face and watches Kaiser work the perimeter of the buildings. The dog is about as good a guardian as Jay could have. No wonder Sister Clare lets the boy live up here; he is probably safer here than any other place—as long as Kaiser is with him.

A bleary-eyed Sister Clare, in a long woolen nightgown, patiently escorts Jay to the porch and interrupts his dialogue with the command for him to wait there until she invites him in. As Ethan approaches with a small wooden bucket filled with water, the nun glares at him. Knowing that the end of her peaceful slumber must have been jarring, Ethan again feels better about how he woke up.

"Thought you might like some fresh water for your morning wash." Ethan's voice is chipper, and his eyes twinkle mischievously.

"How thoughtful." Sister Clare notices he finds the situation humorous. She suspects he may have asked Jay to wake her up. "Hopefully you had nothing to do with the rather rude awakening I experienced."

"No stopping him, ma'am." Ethan's smile betrays his amusement.

"I shall not be long." Sister Clare's eyes soften, and she returns his smile.

"Do what you need, Sister. Jay and I will take a look around the barn. We will come in and fix a meal when you're ready."

Sister Clare insists on helping with breakfast and manages to serve the thinnest flapjacks and most watered-down coffee he has ever tasted. The bacon is so burned it crumbles upon touch. Ethan earlier thought this might be their last good meal, but now he cannot wait to be cooking on his own. An amusing thought enters his mind. *Maybe her lack of cooking and other domestic skills is the real reason she became a nun.* Knowing a smile might elicit a question from Sister Clare about her cooking, he quickly rises from the table. Ethan is gathering his cup and plate for cleaning when Sister Clare clears her throat and addresses him.

"Agreed, Ethan. I will give you a one-day warning."

"I'll load the wagon and hitch up the big hoss. Now, if you don't mind me asking, when are you heading back?"

"I was hoping today, but I am not expected until tomorrow."

"How you getting back?"

Sister Clare stops, a perplexed expression betraying her confusion.

"Why, I hadn't...." Glancing at Ethan, knowing he has caught her in a mistake, she straightens her shoulders. With as much dignity as she can muster, she announces, "I have no recourse except to walk."

The little nun is so ridiculously proud Ethan cannot help himself. His thin smile develops into a grin, then he laughs, a merry, infectious laugh that Sister Clare cannot help but join in.

"My, but that is poor planning on my part," Sister Clare manages as she loses her defensive posture. "I suppose it will be a just punishment for my display of false pride."

"Might be, but if you don't mind, I think I have a better plan. I've checked the tools. Jay's pa kept his implements in good shape. It will be seven days of cutting and raking before Jay and I have the hay dry enough to stack. The rick yards need repair, so ten days in all. After we set up at the hay field, you can take the wagon until then."

"What about borrowing your horse instead?"

"I might let you, but he wouldn't."

"He could tell the difference?"

"Yes, ma'am. If you want to take the chance, I won't stand in your way, but Jay and I have enough to do without caring for your broken bones."

"I will take the wagon," Sister Clare says, smiling, "and leave your particular horse to his peculiar rider."

Ethan's laugh is so genuine that again she cannot help but again join in. It has been a while since she laughed so much, and Sister Clare finds she is enjoying the experience.

Why is there such a lack of merriment in her life? Self-in-flicted somberness? She wonders what it is about this man, this outlaw, that brings out her appreciation of being alive—the simple goodness of it, like laughter.

"Very well, though I may not deserve it." Sister Clare continues to laugh. "Ten days it will be. I will bring Jay more supplies when I return."

Ethan thinks her smile one of the most attractive things he has seen in quite a time.

"Out of curiosity, Sister, what happened to the sheep? Those shears are dull, and that loom in the corner of the house hasn't been used for a few years."

"When Frank, Jay's father, became ill, the Pebet family helped with the livestock until it became obvious there would be no recovery. We knew Jay couldn't run the ranch, so we sold off the stock. The Pebets purchased a large share. They were good friends of the Morgans. The loom hasn't been used since Jay's mother passed away."

"Pebets are the Basque folks north of your mission?"

"Yes."

"Seem like good folks. Kaiser visits their lady dog on occasion."

Sister Clare blushes slightly. Not wanting Ethan to think he can embarrass her, she responds, "They are good people and there are many reasons to visit their ranch."

"Okay, then, Sister. I'll start loading up."

Two scythes and three pitchforks, a stocked tool kit including claw and peen hammers and pliers, and an array of saws hanging in neat rows win Ethan's admiration. Frank Morgan's reputation as a good rancher is reflected in how he kept the place. The tools are well used and well kept. Ethan and Jay push the wagon into the yard and commence loading the implements Ethan thinks they will need. He errs on the side of taking too much rather than being found wanting. The one item he worries about is nails. He suspects the two small rick yards the Apaches use will need repair, and there is only one box of two-inch nails to be found.

"Can I pack my bedroll and closhe now?" Jay asks.

"I think so."

Ethan surveys the eastern landscape. That is where they will come from. Based on Sister Clare's description, he surmises Rufe Harris to be a lazy man who, like most bullies, only picks fights with weaker folks and even then wants others to carry the heavy load for him. That is why he apparently hired a gun, a white-haired man with pale skin to match. Ethan has tried to match the description to any of the gunmen he knows of, but so far cannot come up with any names. Must be someone new to the territory or to the profession. In any case, it pays to know who you're dealing with, and Ethan suspects he will soon find out. He guesses Rufe, confident that he will be unopposed, will sleep in and enjoy a big breakfast before riding out. If coming from town, they should be arriving about three hours after sun-up.

Ethan positions the wagon with the tailgate away from the front porch. The ranch house is where the action will take place, and he wants the wagon to shield him and give him time to act. Placing his rifle on the tailgate behind a stack of tools, Ethan strolls around the front yard, examining the wagon. Imagining the men would stay in the saddle, he rearranges the tools until satisfied that regardless of whether they are on foot or on horse, the rifle will be hidden from their view.

The three horsemen finally appear, riding through the tall meadow grass toward the ranch. Admittedly, Ethan will miss this part of his profession, taking the measure of people and predicting their behavior. On the other hand, Naki-Chaa warns constantly that if he stays in this business too long, he will start to believe everyone acts on dark motives and base instincts. If he begins to think people are all like that, he might become the mean and soulless type he detests. That is why he sent Naki-Chaa west to prepare their secret place. After his job with Old Man Todd, he was supposed to lay up and then head straight there. Now he's stepped into this situation because of a defenseless kid and, God help him, a woman he is trying to impress. *What are you thinking, Ethan?*

Ethan delays hitching the Belgian up until after the expected confrontation takes place. Both horses are safer in their stables where only a stray shot can harm them. Ethan leaves his gun belt off, draped over the stall door near his horse. He knows Sister Clare has been watching him to make sure he remains unarmed. Now that the riders are within hailing distance, Ethan saunters from the barn with his bedroll in his left hand and a scythe casually resting on his right shoulder. Just a hired man taking tools any hay-cutter would pack, going to work in the high country. Ethan acts out a surprised double take at the riders, pretending to notice them for the first time.

"Good morning." Ethan raises his voice short of a shout in a friendly manner. "Think the coffee's all gone, but I'll go check."

Ethan times his walk so that he is at the rear of the wagon as the riders reach the water trough. He places the scythe in the bed.

"You'll stay right where you are, mister."

The son has the cocky bark and nervous manner of an untested dog.

"If we want something, we'll help ourselves, see?" Junior pats his holster.

"I'm in place, then." Ethan raises his eyebrows in feigned surprise.

Keeping Junior in his peripheral vision, Ethan takes time to evaluate the white-haired man. Two guns, but only the right-hand holster shows any wear. He is as calm as Junior is fidgety. The pale blue eyes are sizing Ethan up but noticing all the wrong things. Ethan is trying to look the part of the ranch hand he is portraying, gulping and wetting his lips in an anxious manner. Eyes nervously darting between the three riders. He observes White Hair's eyes as they check for and note Ethan's lack of weapons. White Hair gives the wagon bed loaded with farm implements a dismissive glance, making Ethan hope his act has worked. It is obvious White Hair does not recognize Ethan personally and that Ethan does not fit any description the gunman knows of.

Sister Clare marches from the house, and White Hair turns his horse to show Ethan his profile. Ethan now is sure he has been discounted as a threat. If Ethan had been on a job, White Hair's mistake would prove fatal. The young gunfighter, Ethan believes, is new to the profession.

"This isn't a friendly visit, Mr. Harris," the nun says. "Get to it and leave. I've got work to do."

If Sister Clare is nervous, her voice and manner do not betray it. Ethan thinks of a Banty rooster marching into the hen yard with sharp beak and lethal spurs at the ready to protect his territory. Wiping a skillet with a hand towel, she halts in front of Rufe Harris and boldly stares at him. She completely ignores the gunman. She is unafraid, facing a minor threat—more a tiresome nuisance. A thought whispers at Ethan as he watches the defiant nun set her jaw toward the rancher: *She is the type of woman a man wants at his side.*

Ethan steadies his breathing and Ethan steadies his breathing and finally acknowledges what he has resisted since their first meeting: he finds Clare the most attractive woman he has ever met. She is someone he wants to talk to, listen to, be with. A friend, only one he'd like to hold hands with. With a great effort, Ethan pushes the thought into a corner. He has business to attend to.

"Now, look here, Sister," Rufe says. He shifts his weight and tries to take on a casual tone. "Can't a man be neighborly and check up on a friend?"

"You are neither a neighbor nor a friend. You sneak up here from your warehouse through the Smithson ranch. If your intentions were friendly, everyone would know of your visits up here."

"Now Sister Cla—"

"The answer is no, Mr. Harris. The ranch is not for sale."

"Now, that is for the boy to decide, and besides, we just come up to see if we can help out with the hay."

"As you can see, we hired a man to help with the hay. As for the ranch, the boy is a minor and anything he signs will be null and void. Is there anything else?"

White Hair maneuvers his horse between the nun and the house.

"I'd like to do this peaceable-like, but winter is coming, and I think the boy should decide about my offer. My hands could bring in the hay with no problems. I'm willing to pay a fair price for it. Now, where is the boy?"

"Was that a peaceful threat, or is your true nature finally coming out? The hay is not for sale. It has been promised to Ba'cho and his people."

"Now, be reasonable. There is enough for all, and I have cash."

"We are done, Mr. Harris. It is time for you to leave."

"Hey, Shishter Clare." Jay trots from the house. "I done all the dishesh."

Junior turns his horse and rides at Jay. Startled, Jay lets out a yelp. As he skids to a halt, his feet go out from under him, and he lands on his rump. At the same instant, while all other eyes are focused on the boy, Ethan sees a bolt of silver and black hurtle from the shadows of the porch. Looming over Jay, Junior is laughing at him. At full speed, Kaiser leaps through the air at Junior and knocks him from his horse. The dog immediately goes for the throat and Junior barely brings up a protective arm in time to save his life. Anticipating the next move, Ethan springs into action a second before White Hair reaches for his gun.

"Hold it!" Ethan shouts. In one motion, Ethan pulls the rifle from the wagon and fires a shot just over White Hair's right shoulder. His actions have the desired effect; except for Kaiser and Junior, all eyes are on him.

"Help me!" Junior screeches desperately. "He's gonna kill me!"

"You'll be first," Ethan says, nodding toward White Hair. "Two bullets in you before the fat man can even clear leather."

"Pull on him, dammit!" Rufe screams. "What am I paying you for?"

"Not to play a losing hand, Mr. Harris," Ethan calmly answers. He sees White Hair lower the gun into its holster, release the gun handle, and place his hands on the pommel. Keeping his eyes on the gunman, Ethan addresses Sister Clare. "Sister, you and Jay release Kaiser and head back onto the porch. And remember to praise the dog for a job well done."

Sister Clare complies but scowls at Ethan the whole time. The fool man! She could have managed this without violence.

"Now, Mr. Harris, you drop your gun belt and your rifle and get to your son. I want his belt and rifle on the ground also. Any movement to use it, and I'll kill you both." Ethan keeps the rifle pointed at White Hair. "Now," Ethan says to the gunman, "one at a time, empty your chambers, first revolvers and then your gun belt." Ethan notices that White Hair carries no rifle. A sure sign he is not from the territory.

White Hair complies, all the while smiling at Ethan. When finished, the gunman holsters his empty weapons and places his hands back on the pommel. Ethan keeps his rifle aimed at White Hair.

Rufe Harris helps his whimpering son onto his horse.

"Why does he get to keep his guns?" Rufe asks.

"Your guns will be left at the mission with Mother Joachim, though she might not give them back without a confession." Ethan keeps his voice even. "Now, get out and don't come back."

"Enjoy it, 'field hand.'" White Hair continues to smile at Ethan as he adds, "Every dog has his day."

Ethan remains quiet. The "field hand" comment could mean that White Hair is taunting an inferior or that he recognizes the professional courtesy and suspects Ethan is more than he appears. Watching as they make their way toward the wagon trail that leads to town, Ethan gradually relaxes his trigger finger.

"Why *did* you let him keep his weapons?"

Smiling at the sister, Ethan emits a sigh.

"To avoid a gun fight. He wouldn't have given up his tools of the trade. He would have chanced it. I gave him a way out."

Ethan saunters over to Kaiser, who is being examined by Jay.

"Any wounds?"

"No, shir." Jay looks up at Ethan with a worried expression. "Why were they mean?"

Crouching down, Ethan pats the big shepherd.

"Some men are just bad, Jay. You know how there are good things and evil things in the world?"

"Evil like the devil?"

"Yeah, like men who work for the devil. They hire on to get what they want in return for doing his work. Well, that is why they are mean. Kaiser here represents what is good, and the Harris men want evil."

"Jay," Sister Clare interrupts, "you and Kaiser finish packing the food and we can get started. Really, Ethan," she continues after Jay leaves, "you, of all people, giving theological lessons?"

"Well, ma'am, was there anything wrong with…"

"And why did you interfere? I had everything under control."

Ethan stares at the defiant nun. *Everything under control? Is she serious?* Standing righteously before him, fists on her hips, sharp eyes challenging, Sister Clare glares back at him. Ethan decides it is time to confront her. Taking a breath, black brows lowered over hard, serious eyes, Ethan lets out what he has been considering all morning long.

"What happens to that boy when the dog is gone?" Ethan cannot understand how someone as smart as Sister Clare cannot see the obvious. "Contrary to your belief that you are the boy's protector, his survival is dependent on that dog, not you. The same dog that would be dead right now if I wasn't here."

Sister Clare opens her mouth to speak.

"No offense, ma'am, but you really need to rethink how you are going about this. They will be gunning for Kaiser. Without that dog, where is the boy? His future is to be a worker at your mission, without pride and totally at the mercy of your charity. The boy just might have hopes and dreams like everyone else. Those birds aren't finished with him, and they know who really stands between them and Jay now, even if you don't."

Turning away, too angry to converse any longer, Ethan lays his rifle on the wagon seat. Over his shoulder, he tells Sister Clare, "I'm hitching the Belgian. We leave as soon as I'm finished."

Watching the lean man walk to the barn, Sister Clare is reminded of a cougar she once encountered. The cat had eyed her contemptuously as if reminding her she is in his realm, before confidently turning his back on her because he was in charge—and she knew it.

"I'll be ready," she mutters. The man has taken control again. What really annoys her is that he might be right. Time for her to reconsider the entire plan the mission has set out to care for Jay and this ranch.

CHAPTER 8

As expected, there are unshod hoof prints around his camp. Ba'cho must have laid down the law, because Ethan finds nothing missing. He and Jay take down the lean-to and load his belongings into the wagon. He hopes at least some of Ba'cho's men will stick around the high meadows while they are cutting and ricking. He is fairly certain the Apaches have figured out that a feud is playing out between the Morgan and Harris camps. They might give him warning if Rufe and White Hair come back.

"Well, Sister Clare," Ethan says in a congenial tone as he swings down from his mount, "I think this is the spot." The high grass of the open meadow may have been the traditional hay field, or it may have grown high due to lack of grazing. Regardless, it is the right location and quality for what is needed. "Let's unload."

While riding to the meadow, Sister Clare tries to evaluate what Ethan has said, but emotions take control and she grows increasingly angry. *How can he think he can just ride into this situation and believe he has it all figured out? The temerity; no, the arrogance!* Sister Clare crosses her arms and gives him her sternest look.

"We'll set up our camp later." Ethan turns around to locate the nun. "Need to get you on the way before.... Now, that's not the look of somebody pulling up their sleeves to help out."

"I thought we'd finish our conversation."

"No conversation to finish, ma'am. You want to argue, you can do it with the back end of the horse as you head home."

"It would prove, I'm sure, a far more intelligent discussion than I could have with you."

Ethan laughs and slaps his knee in approval.

"And a more pleasant countenance to look at while speaking." Now why did she add that? It is mean spirited, not clever. "I am sorry for that last remark. It is unbecoming."

"No, Sister, it's just fine." Ethan is laughing so hard that he has to lean against the wagon. "Truth be, if I were handsome, some gal would have tried to put the brand on me long ago. Honestly, ma'am, I haven't enjoyed anyone's company this much in a long time."

"Hey, what'sh sho funny?" Jay runs up with Kaiser at his side. "We been exshploring and you been having fun."

"Sister Clare was just reminding me of my attributes." Ethan wipes his eyes. "Time to get to work."

"Before you do—" Embarrassed, Sister Clare shakes her head and sighs. "I am truly sorry for those comments. They are not true and do not represent my feelings. You are, in fact, a handsome man. If I didn't have faith that you are a man of your word, with Jay's best interest at heart, I would not be leaving, or I would be leaving with Jay."

"I understand, ma'am. You think I haven't considered your position? You took on a heavy load when you accepted this responsibility." Ethan wants to ask her what her feelings actually are, but he lets it pass. He is afraid she might take it wrong or, more on the mark, he might be reading more into her comments than she intended. He smiles at her and is gratified at the smile she returns to him. "We better get to work."

As Ethan and Jay strip off their shirts, Sister Clare is struck at how muscular Jay is. The boy is filling out, his shoulders defined and the soft fat of boyhood barely detectable. Maybe Ethan has a point. Turning to Ethan she catches her breath. Old scars crisscross his back. The belt marks meted out by the drunk uncle are still detectable beneath his undershirt and on his bare shoulders. Ethan did not exaggerate. Seeing the remnants of the old wounds, she realizes his uncle really had beaten Ethan almost to death. Yet Ethan has been so matter of fact, as if his harsh young life is unremarkable. What a strange country, at once so breathtakingly beautiful and so brutal.

Sister Clare steps away from the wagon and plops herself onto an old tree stump, lost in thought. Glancing at Ethan, she sees him look up and smile at her. His weathered skin along with his black hair is so typical of the men of the West, yet looking at his profile she is struck by how attractive he is. What would she think of him if she was not aware of his past? But those scars on his back probably match the violent scars on his soul. She notices him glancing at her again before resuming his work. She notes the alert eyes of a predator, narrowed into a permanent squint from the desert sun. Sister Clare is always amazed at how men like Ethan can be so thin yet so strong. Unlike Jay, there is not an ounce of fat discernible, burned off by the heat and the need for quick reactions to survive in this land.

Jay and Ethan laugh at something, and Ethan gives the boy a pat on the shoulder. Sister Clare crosses her legs and chuckles at her confused and contradictory attitude toward this man. Maybe Mother Joachim has a point. If Ethan's story is true, he may have a positive moral compass. He may actually care about Jay. And there is that question: What will happen to Jay in the future?

"Oh, how I sometimes hate self-reflection," she mutters aloud. "The man is right. I have not thought beyond the immediate problem. Dear God!"

CHAPTER 9

Despite the morning excitement, Sister Clare's trip back to the mission is uneventful. She can tell word of the confrontation has not reached town. As she guides the wagon through the dusty street, the voices and expressions of those she encounters are normal and lack any concern or curiosity. She is met by the usual nods and tipped caps and "Afternoon, Sister"'s. Mr. Birnbaum at least notices that she has Jay's wagon and horse.

"You handle that Belgian well, Sister." The stocky man smiles at her. "Boy not with you?"

"He and Kaiser are staying at the ranch. I want Pickles to check the wagon and make any repairs."

Turning the wagon into the mission courtyard, Sister Clare is met by Pickles, the old handyman Mother Joachim hired on years ago for room and board, with an additional two dollars a week. Mother Joachim found Pickles nearly frozen to death as he huddled next to the church. He came to the mission after looking for work at every ranch and business establishment in the area. No one had use for a one-handed man with rolled shoulders, thinning gray hair, and missing teeth. After cleaning him up and learning his history, Mother Superior gave him a job and more respect than Sister Clare thinks he deserves. Sister Clare believes him more interested in telling stories and engaging in idle chatter than work.

"Now that is a fine animal, Sister," Pickles says. He takes the bridle with his hand and strokes the Belgian's neck with his stump. "Morgan's horse and wagon, if I'm not mistaken."

"Yes. Please care for him, then check the wagon and make any repairs it might need. We will be keeping them here for a while."

"Boy not with you? He might be handy helping out."

"No." Sister Clare gives him a perplexed look. Why did he say that?

"Just thinking, ma'am, a fine animal like this needs exercise. May I see to it while he's our guest?"

"Yes." Sister Clare watches the man unhitch the horse, all the while complimenting and then conversing with the beast. *Dear Lord,* she thinks, *you put those words in his mouth. Is this Jay's future?*

"Mother Joachim, may I enter?" After seeing the nodding assent, Sister Clare takes the offered seat. She has freshened up, if changing her habit and washing her face and hands and then her feet in a basin counts for that. Cleaning her feet and putting on fresh hose may seem little to most women, but it is something that rejuvenates her body and spirits like nothing else. Sister Clare thought it might be sinful, but both Mother Joachim and Father Joseph assured her that it is a natural and healthy act.

"Well, Sister Clare." Mother Joachim puts her ledger away and smiles at her young protégé. "What did you discover?"

"As I suspected, he is an outlaw. A rather dangerous one at that."

"What is his name?"

"I cannot disclose it at this time."

Noticing Mother Joachim's expression quickly transform from concern to alarm to anger, Sister Clare holds up her hands and makes her posture as supplicating as possible.

"I mean no disrespect. I am sure you will understand if I may tell the entire story before you ask any questions of me."

Unclenching her fists and leaning back in the chair, Mother Joachim nods. "Proceed."

Sister Clare leaves nothing out, from her arrival on the meadow until leaving the hay-cutting camp—except Ethan's true identity and his history. Mother Joachim drums her finger atop the desk, then asks her to repeat in detail the encounter with Ba'cho and the confrontation with Rufe Harris. Additionally, the Mother Superior takes great interest in not only Ethan's physical description, but that of his horse. Despite the probing, Sister Clare feels she acquits herself well in both performing her duty to the mission and keeping her promise to Ethan.

Staring out the window, Mother Joachim suppresses a smile. *Oh, you are capable my young friend, but not nearly as clever as you think. About six foot tall, dark in skin and hair, lightening reactions, rides a gray mustang with spots on the rump, and has the respect of a man like Ba'cho; what gunman is as adept with rifle and handgun and knows the way of the Apache? There is only one man in the territory who fits that description.* Sister Clare has made no mention of the scar under the chin, but there is little question of the man's identity. Mother Joachim has never met or seen the man, but it has to be him. Sister Clare has met Apache Jack.

Smiling benignly, Mother Joachim considers the situation. Sister Clare, as absolutist a person as she has met, left Jay in the care and under the protection of Apache Jack. Everything she has heard of the man's good qualities must be true. For him to have convinced Sister Clare of his trustworthiness—well, that speaks volumes.

Glancing at Sister Clare, the Mother Superior considers the irony. *You just may have done better than you think, my young friend. I need to put aside all of this paperwork and get out like I used to.* No doubt about it: Sister Clare met someone who isn't intimidated by her, yet by all accounts treats her with respect and deference. But that begs the question. It makes sense for someone on the run to choose a remote place like the Morgan ranch, but why is he going out of his way to help Jay?

"I hope you are not displeased."

Mother Joachim wants to laugh at the question. Sister Clare cares little about "displeasing" her Mother Superior. She is still as righteous and self-assured as ever, except it has been Apache—no, Ethan who took on the job of cutting the hay without prodding or negotiating. They aren't even paying him.

"These men often live by a code of honor, almost an Old Testament type of morality, where justice is meted out according to each individual's sense of right and wrong," Mother Joachim muses aloud. "Jay may be safer now, with this Ethan, than since his father died."

"That brings me to another matter." Sister Clare takes a deep breath. Admitting she may have been remiss in her decision while in charge of Jay's welfare will be acknowledging a shortcoming. But how will the Mother Superior, just as complicit in the plan, react to being questioned about it? "What happens when Kaiser can no longer protect Jay?"

"Well, he comes to live here. Pickles can certainly use the help."

"So that is to be his future." Sister Clare allows the resignation in her voice to have a bitter edge.

Blinking her eyes in astonishment, Mother Joachim opens her mouth to speak but is at a loss. The girl has managed to trump her. What have they been doing? Cleverly managing the estate just as Jay's father desired, but not considering the human being at the center of it. Convicted! They lost sight of the most important issue: Jay.

"I will not be false, Mother Superior. I was reminded of this duty, this foremost duty, by the outlaw Ethan."

Mother Joachim faces the young nun at the use of her title. Sister Clare is contrite, sincere in the admission. The outlaw, the gunman, the savage has proved a better caretaker than they.

"We have been humbled." Mother Joachim chuckles softly. "Come with me to the chapel where we will make our confession and pray for the strength and wisdom to do better. Tomorrow we will regroup."

CHAPTER 10

"So why didn't you go for your gun?" Rufe spits out the words.

White Hair remains mounted. He prefers to stay in town at Rufe's warehouse. The main house and outbuildings of the Harris ranch are scattered along a hot and dusty bluff. From White Hair's observation, there is no rational plan for any of the structures. The house sits between two barns and the bunkhouse is next door, with corrals scattered haphazardly throughout. It appears that when something is needed, it is built without any concern for function and utility. White Hair was raised on a ranch and knows the purpose and function of every building and tool. Here, if the intent has been to make everything inconvenient and the work harder to perform, Harris has succeeded. The gunman hates the place and is developing a dislike for the people who live and work there as well.

"I did."

"Who did you pull on?" Junior snarls.

The cockiness has returned to Junior Harris. The gashes on his left arm still ooze blood through the bandanna Rufe has used for a bandage. After moaning for half the trip home, Junior let his anger take over, and vows of revenge were shouted through forest and canyon. The gunman wants to tell him to shut up, but Junior is so distraught he might do something stupid, like pick a fight.

"The most dangerous one there: the dog."

"So why didn't you kill him?" Junior turns and confronts the gunman.

"There was a Winchester pointed at me by someone who looked like he knew his business."

"You was scared of a field hand?" Junior sneers.

Leaning back in the saddle, White Hair smiles grimly and drops his right arm. Junior is lucky he framed it as a question. White Hair stares at the youth, daring him to say more. He has observed Junior since their first meeting and finds the man to be cruel. Creating fear and the threat of violence is part of a gunman's trade, but Junior takes delight in the pain and suffering and torture of death. White Hair would like an excuse to rid the world of Junior Harris.

Rufe quickly steps between them and shoves Junior toward the house.

"You go get that tended to by Billy. Get in there, I tell you, and have Billy patch you up."

"I ain't scared" are Junior's parting words.

"He meant nothing by that," Rufe adds reassuringly. "You not getting down?"

"Heading back to town. I want to make some inquiries about that 'hired hand.'"

"Oh, he's just some no account the sisters took on to be a caretaker."

"I don't think so. He handled himself like he knew his business."

"You're just upset because he surprised us. Do you think the nuns hired a gun?" Rufe barks a laugh. "It's Sister Clare and that old witch, Mother Joachim, we need to outsmart. You just keep the ranchers like Smithson and the rest in their place, and I'll have that ranch by spring."

"All the same," White Hair says, swinging his horse around and starting toward town, "I'm going to find out who the hired man is."

"Ah, don't worry about him, I tell you."

CHAPTER 11

The windrows are far from straight. Stepping atop a boulder, Ethan can see that they curve in great arcs across the meadow. Both he and Jay are right-handed and the first swath of cut grass bent left, so all the others follow suit. Five days of cutting is hard work, with blisters and sharpening dull blades and replacing the shoulder padding and falling so deep asleep that their snoring has probably driven all the game from the high country. By the time Ethan decides there is enough for the Apaches and Jay's winter needs, the grass proves dry enough to rake. That takes less time than expected, and now the curved windrows of the mown hay cover a good portion of the meadow, ready for the next task of transporting to the rick yards and barn. Jumping from the rock to where Jay is leaning on his pitchfork, Ethan pats the boy on the back and nods in approval. It is all done and ready to stack.

Jay has proved a good worker. The boy is obviously used to helping out, as Ethan learns not just from Jay's hard labor but from his constant chatter. Ethan would bet the house that Jay left nothing out from his life history, and now the Morgans have no secrets left because of it. Which is a good reminder for Ethan to watch what he says and does with Jay nearby: if given the chance, the boy will relate anything he hears in detail to anyone who asks. Still, Ethan is glad he heard it all, the highlights and the mundane. Jay has given a good account of the man and woman who had made a life here in the high country. Perhaps it did not end as they hoped; certainly Jay isn't the child they expected. But they had been good people, and maybe things would turn out well for what they left behind. Naki-Chaa has a saying: *The "Special Ones" are close to God, so have a care how you treat them.*

The only thing missing is the wagon. It has been nine days, and Sister Clare is due back. Ethan thinks of her, too often and in the wrong way, but it is one of those subjects that proves hard to keep out of his thoughts. Especially when it provides a missing piece in his plans. Forty-five acres of land; Ethan can see the flat where the new orchards will be, rolling up and around the oak studded hill. That hill is where he will build the house. Naki-Chaa should have the foundations for the stable and barn outlined by the time he arrives. The Gravensteins they planted in the first orchard might even produce a crop next year. The trees will be four years old by then, but Naki-Chaa is the expert, while Ethan is still learning.

"Hey, Ethan, what we doin' today?"

"How about a picnic."

"Really?"

"Why not? Can't finish without the wagon. I'll fashion a pole. I bet I can land a few trout for lunch."

"You think you really can?"

"Done it before," Ethan laughs. "The beaver pond is full of them. Afterward, you can jump in the water."

"Oh, boy, shwimming!"

True to his word, Ethan takes the creel from his saddlebag, finds a likely branch for his rod, and chooses a likely fly. Within minutes of his first cast, he lands two trout. They are on the small side but big enough to eat. Ethan cleans the catch and throws the remains into the middle of the pond. After building a fire, they cook the fish and eat. Kaiser joins them just as the last bite is taken.

"Hey, Kaisher, where you been?"

"He's been hunting." Ethan points to the red fur around the dog's mouth. "What do you think? Rabbit or squirrel? Or maybe a mole?"

"Shaw him get a groush once. Had feathersh my pa had to pick out of his teeth. Can I go in the water now?"

"Sure."

"Oh, boy!"

As Jay runs to the water, leaving a trail of clothing in his wake, Ethan leans back against a tree trunk and gazes across the pond and over the trees. It occurs to him that he doesn't know whether or not Jay can swim. What the hell— he can pull the boy out if he flounders.

"Hey, Kaisher, come on in," Jay yells.

The dog sits, looks at Ethan with an expression that conveys how ridiculous he thinks humans are, and then lies on his stomach while keeping watch over Jay.

"I won't argue the point, Kaiser."

Leaning back, Ethan closes his eyes and begins to daydream. He has always saved his earnings, first in the money belt he wore, next in a bank at Santa Fe, finally with Naki-Chaa. No one ever knew the old crippled Indian had more cash hidden away than some of the wealthiest men in the territory. The two of them have planned and saved and hunted for the right place, and he has finally found it. Now he can stop dreaming about his future and start living it. Yet not quite. There is one thing missing: a woman. He dares to dream he can have that, too—and, in this unlikeliest place, he has met the unlikeliest of candidates. She is everything he desires in a woman: strong, smart, spirited and pretty. But she is a nun. *Is it wrong?*

Ethan opens his eyes upon hearing an unnatural sound behind him. The stirring of pine needles or scuff of a toe on loose dirt, about forty feet back. Ethan remains in his casual position but keeps an eye on the shepherd. When he sees the dog's ears come forward, he knows someone is watching them. A few moments later, observing Kaiser still tracking the sound but relaxed in posture, Ethan knows who it is.

"There is no fish left," Ethan comments laconically.

"That is too bad." Ba'cho steps forward and squats next to Ethan. "The grass is ready."

"All we need is the wagon."

"There is a man asking about you, Cactus. Now others know someone is here with Jay Morgan."

"I figured they would. We had a scrape with the Harris folks."

"Are you staying?"

"Plan on pulling out after the hay is in."

"They will kill the wolf dog, and there will be no protection for Jay Morgan."

Ethan stares over the treetops at the puffs of cotton gathering in the sky.

"You saved Naki-Chaa. It is said he is at your home far in the West."

Ethan takes a deep breath. God help him, but he has thought about this very thing for the past ten days. It is obvious the nuns have no long-term plans; they probably won't be able to really understand Jay's needs. He may be a "Special One," but even Jay will finally figure out how things stand. After being crippled, Naki-Chaa had been straightforward: he was going into the desert to die. "At least I will have the dignity of providing food for the scavengers," he said. To waste away at the mercy of others was too bitter a future for a proud man like Naki-Chaa.

It was the promise of partnering with Ethan in the farm that gave Naki-Chaa a reason to live. It had been an easy sell; Ethan really does need him. Ethan trusts him and leaves him in charge of the farm and money—basically, he has Ethan's future in his hands. And Naki-Chaa pulls his weight. His knowledge of fruit trees and orchards and grafting is critical for success; therefore, having him as a partner makes sense. Taking on Jay? Naki-Chaa is an asset, but Jay would be a lifetime responsibility, and that is a huge difference.

"You can make your dwelling big enough for another."

His house would be large enough for another, but for someone Ethan will choose to share his life. How can he ask a woman to share a life that includes caring for Jay?

"Will you look in on him after I'm gone?"

"The winter is short, Cactus. I am Apache, and your laws do not allow my people to harm white men, even to protect a Special One. If he stays, I do not expect to see him here when we return next year."

"Are we responsible for every stray in the world?"

"Maybe only the strays that find us."

Ethan drops his head and closes his eyes.

"Take care, wolf dog." Ba'cho nods respectfully to Kaiser.

CHAPTER 12

Looping the reins around the hitching rail, the gunman pats the shoulder of his horse and steps onto the saloon porch. He pauses to let his eyes adjust to the dark interior before stepping through the doors. Removing his hat, he brushes back his white hair. He has stopped at every ranch and establishment on his way into town to ask about the hired hand at the Morgan spread. Nobody even knew that someone was working the Morgan place, much less had a clue as to his identity. Most referred him to the mission folk—who would know, of course—but that is the one place he doesn't stop to inquire.

"Rye," the gunman says as he lays a silver coin on the bar.

"Here you go." The barkeep places a half-filled bottle and shot glass in front of the gunman. "You want change? That's more than what's left in the bottle."

"No, you keep it. Would like some information."

"If I have it to give."

"You know anything about a hired man up at the Morgan place?"

"News to me."

"No one come through asking for work?"

"They usually would stop in here, mister, yet the truth is I haven't had anybody ask about work since about month or so ago. Sent him on to Prescott."

"What did he look like?"

"About up to your shoulders, a little round in the middle, sort of like me but without the mustache. Looked more like a shopkeeper than a cowhand."

The gunman walks to a corner table and sits with his back to a wall. No one has seen the man, and yet there he is. It didn't figure. If he is a professional, why would he take on the job of a hired hand? And would the old padre and sisters at the mission hire a gun? Maybe Rufe is right. But the man handled that Winchester like he knew the business. It just doesn't add up.

CHAPTER 13

Even from a distance, the little caravan strikes Ethan as comical. No need for concern about trouble from this group. A man sits on the wagon bench driving. Despite having only one hand, he appears to manage the big Belgian quite well. The horse looks well fed and groomed, in better shape than when he left. Just to the front of the wagon are two nuns riding sidesaddle. One rides upright and observant, pointing and nodding and obviously engaging in conversation, mostly with the wagon driver. The other sister slumps in her saddle, a resigned posture conveying to the world her displeasure. Ethan laughs aloud. So the Mother Superior has come to investigate, and poor Sister Clare is relegated to second fiddle.

"Well, it appears your outlaw has given you a fair week of work," Mother Joachim observes with approval. "In fact, I would say his production is exemplary."

"Lot of hay to be ricked for sure," Pickles agrees before spitting a stream of tobacco juice over the side of the buckboard.

Usually, Mother Joachim detests the habit of tobacco in any form, but she knows Sister Clare is even more intolerant. She watches the young nun grip the pommel and glare in disgust at Pickles. Is she actually engaged in mentoring by example or enjoying Sister Clare wallow in her petulance?

Shrugging, Mother Joachim keeps up her happy demeanor and smiles at the handyman.

"Another reason why you are here, Pickles." Mother Joachim can almost hear the younger nun's teeth grinding. "Why, Sister Clare, is that your outlaw friend waving to us? And here comes that dog from the trees. Now, why do you suppose he isn't with Jay and the outlaw?"

"He has been shadowing us for the last half mile," Sister Clare remarks in an exasperated tone, "if you hadn't noticed."

"You're good, Sister Clare." Pickles cackles. "I hadn't even caught that. You'd have made a good Army Scout."

Sister Clare glances at Mother Joachim and rolls her eyes.

When Mother Joachim decided she would accompany Sister Clare to investigate the situation at the Morgan ranch for herself, she knew Sister Clare would protest and be unpleasant company; her prediction has proved correct. Sister Clare is quite capable, and normally she would have let the young nun handle things. It is Apache Jack and the confrontation with Rufe Harris that changed things. As Mother Superior, she believes it her duty to investigate such a serious matter personally. Besides, she wants to meet this Apache Jack, though she must be sure to use his assumed name. *Actually*, she reflects, *Ethan might even be his real name.* Apache Jack. Even the toughest warriors and hardened scouts spoke of him with respect. In any event, Sister Clare's pride has been hurt, and that prevents anything constructive from being discussed, let alone decided, between them. Maybe it is just as well; she can assess the situation for herself before a plan is made. Besides, watching Sister Clare in a foul temper proves more amusing than she imagined. It is like dealing with the teenaged daughter she would never have, or perhaps imagining her own mother navigating her growth from girl to woman.

"Sister Clare, I think it would be best if you take the lead on dealing with this situation."

"Why pretend?" Sister Clare replies, shrugging her shoulders.

"Call it what you will, but do you not think it makes sense? You have the stronger relationship with the boy and are the only one who has even met this Ethan. It has to be you."

In reply, Sister Clare kicks her mount into a trot.

Hearing Pickles emit a soft chuckle, Mother Joachim allows herself to join in.

"Best not make a habit of laughing at her, Pickles. She will have you for breakfast and spit you out at lunch."

"That be the truth," Pickles agrees. "That is one tough woman."

Mother Joachim's original plan is to make a brief on sight analysis of the outlaw, inspect the physical state of the house and outbuildings, and be back at the mission before nightfall. Her assessment, based on Sister Clare's report, is colored by her confidence in the young nun's abilities but tempered by her own responsibilities, including a promise to a dying man. Plans might change, so she prepared overnight bags just in case.

Halting her mount in front of Ethan, Sister Clare dismounts before he can help her down. They face each other, but Sister Clare keeps her eyes fixed on the tree line over his head. Admitting to the man that he is right will be difficult. She lowers her eyes to his, and everything she has planned to say vanishes. Ethan's expression is warm and welcoming.

"We missed you, Sister Clare."

Ethan's smile is genuine. He means every word. His body language indicates—or, at least, Sister Clare suspects—that he will return a hug if she offers. The man is actually glad to see her.

"The Mother Superior, Mother Joachim, has come to inspect your work, and I have come to return the horse and wagon," she announces awkwardly.

"And it's a pleasure to see you again, too," Ethan replies. "Actually sorry we let you go. Could have used the help."

"Let me go?" Sister Clare responds incredulously. Regaining her balance, she brings her clenched fists to her hips. "I left because I decided it was the proper thing to do!"

"Well, in any case, it is real nice to see you again, Sister Clare. We did miss having you here."

Sister Clare exhales, her body suddenly relaxed. He has done it again! Totally disarmed her. Her emotions hit hills and valleys whenever she deals with him. How can the man be so commanding in every situation?

"Hey, Shishter Clare, guesh what we got to do yeshterday!"

Sister Clare watches as Ethan saunters over to the Mother Superior. Jay rattles on, relating every detail of the fishing and swimming holiday. Sister Clare faces the boy and cannot help but break into a grin as Jay's infectious joy overwhelms her. For once, it is easy to listen to Jay as he relates the wonderful ten days he has spent with his new friend, the gunfighter, outlaw, killer of men, Apache Jack. *What a strange situation: the fate of lives depending on this man. What is the right path going forward? Dear God, what a dilemma.*

"You must be Ethan," Mother Joachim says, smiling.

"Guilty as charged, ma'am," Ethan says with a nod.

His lean face carries the creases and worn leather color that mark long exposure to the desert climate. The eyes, while narrowed against the grit-filled wind of the southwest, are wide enough for Mother Joachim to read the man's hope and delight. Holding out her hand, she feels a firm but respectful grip. When he raises his head, she sees the scar just under his chin; it's hard to see under the stubble of whiskers, but there nonetheless. From every description of Apache Jack given by those who have met him, it is *the* distinguishing mark to identify the outlaw.

"You don't look as fearsome as I expected," Ethan says, then he grins at her.

But you are every bit the dangerous puma I expected, she wants to reply. Lean but muscular, every nerve taut and quick, ready to switch from relaxed and casual to explosive action in a heartbeat; Apache Jack is as impressive in person as his formidable reputation. Yet those eyes display the joy of youth! There is no mistaking that, regardless of what hardships he has endured, the man still loves life.

"I am not in charge here." Mother Joachim nods toward the younger nun. "You need to deal with Sister Clare. That, Ethan, might prove more fearsome than dealing with me."

"I think Sister Clare and I have a good measure of one another. A pleasure meeting you, ma'am." Ethan tips his hat.

Interesting how he said that, Mother Joachim muses. She watches as he approaches Sister Clare. The young nun is attempting to examine the hay field while a wildly gesticulating Jay dances around her.

"You be wanting to get down, Sister?" Pickles asks.

"Not yet." She likes her vantage point atop her horse.

"Think I best be getting this here wagon over there so they can start loading."

The situation is just as Sister Clare described it. Jay's body is developing into manhood, with all the attendant difficulties that maturity will bring. Mentally he might forever be a boy, but physically he is becoming an adult. What about emotionally? Will they be the best guardians? He will never be able to provide for himself, but what can the mission provide besides room and board and the odd jobs the boy can handle? And putting aside the inevitability of the dog dying, what happens when she and Sister Clare are dead or transferred? Who will understand the history of Jay?

Noticing Sister Clare arch a questioning eyebrow at her, she shrugs her shoulders and shakes her head.

"I have no good answer," Mother Joachim says softly, knowing she cannot be heard.

Nodding her head that she understands, Sister Clare manages to smile.

Yes, Mother Joachim muses, *you've made your point. The solution you've proposed is another matter.* This Ethan *is* Apache Jack, with all the baggage his reputation carries. Leaving the boy in his charge for a month or two is one thing, but.... No, there has to be a better solution. Still, just look at how he and Jay get along. No patronizing or even paternal displays by Ethan. It is like watching an older brother with a much younger sibling. The man does have a way with people. Even Pickles is smiling while he works. They all seem to be enjoying themselves, and Ethan is at the center of the activity. Even with Sister Clare marching around and pointing and ordering, it is Ethan who is really in charge. Does she see it? He defers to her with a nod and a smile, then they all continue to work as if she is not there, Pickles slowly driving the wagon along the windrows while Ethan and Jay fork the hay onto the wagon bed.

With the hay beginning to spill over the sides, Ethan jumps into the wagon bed to tamp down and balance the load. After finishing, he smiles down at the young nun.

"How does it look, boss?"

"It will do," the nun says as she walks from the rear of the wagon toward the front.

Leaping from the wagon, Ethan almost lands on Sister Clare.

"Good heavens, woman, get out of the way!" Mother Joachim mutters to herself. "Do you not notice he isn't paying—good Lord, it is I who have not been paying attention!"

"Whoa there, Sister Clare." Ethan sees her at the last second and barely manages to put an extra effort in his push-off to miss landing atop her. Alighting next to her, Ethan uses her shoulder to steady himself. "Sorry, ma'am," he says, gently squeezing her shoulder. "Thought you were still behind the wagon."

"For a man with your reputation, I would have thought you might be more observant," Sister Clare admonishes quietly with a gentle smile.

"You have me there, ma'am. I guess we should always be ready for the unexpected."

"Looks like we have enough to take to the rickyard, Ethan," Pickles calls out.

"Lead the way, Jay." Ethan points his hat toward the yard.

"Come on, Kaisher, we'll show 'em."

If the amount and condition of the hay has pleasantly surprised Sister Clare, the rickyard is a revelation. Ethan has used the lumber from the barn to replace all of the fence rails. He also has repaired and raised the surface in the yard, allowing for better drainage. One section of the fence rails has been left unattached and therefore easily slides open to allow access.

"Should keep the deer out, but it won't really." Ethan grins at the young nun.

"Why not?"

"They'll jump right over it. It could be six feet high, and I wouldn't guarantee they couldn't get in."

"Impressive."

"The deer or the rickyard?"

"Both." Sister Care laughs.

"Hear that, Jay? She approves our work!"

"Oh, boy, Ethan, that meansh I won the bet and get to go shwimmin' again."

"It certainly does, Jay."

After forking the last of the hay from the wagon, Ethan lays the pitchfork in the bed and jumps down.

"All right, Pickles," Ethan says as he wipes his brow, "let's get another load."

"What bet?" Sister Clare asks curiously.

"Uh, well." Ethan winces. "We bet that you wouldn't compliment us about our work."

"Really?" Sister Clare smiles sweetly at Ethan while cocking her head.

Ethan turns red as he looks down and kicks at the ground.

Pickles cackles loudly and puts the big Belgian in motion.

"Uh, Sister, we still have a lot to do." Ethan pauses, her smile throwing him so off balance that he cannot look at her. "Be lucky to get it all in by tomorrow night."

"Well, then you better get working before you get into more mischief than betting." Sister Clare is pleased at having the advantage. It is interesting how the man is suddenly acting like a shy schoolboy.

"You all staying at the ranch house?"

"No, we have work at the mission requiring our attention. Pickles will stay to help."

"Appreciate it. He appears to know how to handle that wagon. Now, Sister Clare, those clouds are gathering and have me a little worried about thunderstorms. This time of year they can come unexpected like."

"Mother Joachim and I will take our leave. I am sure we can handle any trouble."

"I'm certain of that." Ethan notices her twinkling eyes and satisfied smile. "I meant no offense by that bet."

"I am sure you did not." She laughs merrily. "I will return in four or five days."

"I look forward to it, Sister."

CHAPTER 14

The Mother Superior allows Sister Clare to take the lead on the ride back to the mission. When asked her thoughts, she tells the younger nun that she needs a little time to sort out everything she has seen and heard. All too true! Mother Joachim never has been confronted with an issue like this. How in the world can it be? Sister Clare is as sharp and observant as anyone Mother Joachim has met but seems oblivious to the fact Apache Jack is smitten with her.

It takes the first couple of miles for Mother Joachim to review all of the evidence, observed and inferred, to confirm that the man is romantically interested in Sister Clare. Appraising her young protégé, Mother Joachim cannot understand it. With her fierce black eyes, Sister Clare reminds Mother Superior of a falcon, often with a disposition to match. Yes, she is young and intelligent, but attractive to a man like Ethan? It is hard to believe. Yet the man could barely keep his eyes off her.

Mother Joachim observed Ethan's long looks at Sister Clare, how his hard face softened as he watched her, often followed by a resigned sigh or a determined shake of the head. That love of life she detects in the man's eyes means he has dreams. Sister Clare mentioned that he is traveling west and alludes to his having a ranch someplace. What does a man with a place to call home dream of? *Heaven help you, Sister Clare,* Mother Joachim thinks, *but you have become a part of his dreams.*

"We are at the main road." Sister Clare's declaration breaks into her thoughts.

"Yes, I see."

"No, you didn't." The young nun laughs and says, "You have been deep in thought the last couple hours. We could have been waylaid and robbed, and you wouldn't have noticed."

"I suppose you are right." Mother Joachim notices how often Sister Clare smiles ever since she was placed in charge at the meadow. Is it that she is in command, or that she was with Ethan? It is nice to be back on a civil footing with the girl, but the cause of Sister Clare's change of attitude happened the moment her Mother Superior stepped away and allowed her to resume the relationship with Ethan and Jay that had developed when they were all alone. That is the issue, isn't it? Her protégé never has acted as congenial and,, well, happy as she is right now. *What happened up there between them? Did they even know? What if....*

"Well, Mother? Your thoughts?"

Mother Joachim clears her throat. *You would be quite surprised at my thoughts* is how she wants to respond.

"Your assessment of the man," Mother Joachim begins, "is correct. Whatever his past, he has a moral compass that makes him trustworthy, at least in this situation." The trick is to watch Sister Clare's every move and listen to her words while noting each inflection. "These western men are interesting, don't you think?"

"I never considered it before I met Ethan." Sister Clare cocks her head in consideration and smiles. "He is the most interesting man I have ever met."

Mother Joachim feels her mouth go dry at the response and waits for Sister Clare to continue.

"With the short time I have had to think on it, I believe this whole culture is founded on the belief of 'free will.' The individual is judged completely on his own merits. Just consider the relationship between Ba'cho and Ethan and Jay. They share a basic sense of 'right and wrong' but share little in upbringing and education."

"You have the basis of a good treatise, Sister Clare." Mother Joachim's response is careful and measured. The girl's enthusiasm is for her thoughts, not for any of the subjects involved. Mother Joachim feels relieved, but not completely. Sister Clare finds the man interesting, and that can often take one down an unexpected path. "So are all of Ethan's past acts true to his code of truth? And, if so, were they justified?"

"Killing is wrong, Mother."

"Is it? Yet we justify self-defense and defending the weak from aggression. Would you defend Jay if he were attacked?"

"With my life, but I don't think I could kill."

"Then your Ethan would argue there would be two dead bodies instead of one. Your effort would only produce the additional horror of Jay seeing a loved one butchered before he is in turn killed."

The younger nun's mouth opens in quick response, but just as quickly clamps shut. Sister Clare pauses and looks quizzically at the older nun.

"I have no ready answer to that," Sister Clare responds, "but there is more to this discussion than morality issues."

"I disagree. It is all about morality."

Mother Joachim grins, and after a pause Sister Clare laughs.

"So where has this got us, Mother? Do you agree we cannot provide the best life for Jay?"

"Yes."

"And that Ethan is like a second father?"

"No. Haven't you noticed? Ethan is a young man but mature beyond his age. He is, as you described, the epitome of the virile western man." She watches Sister Clare's response. No blushing; her eyes remain up and considering; there is no squirming or discomfort that Mother Joachim can detect. "An older brother, perhaps?"

"Yes." Sister Clare looks Mother Joachim in the eye. "That is correct. With all the protective instincts and amusing familiarity an older brother will display."

"A man with the qualities of a good father, brother, husband, friend." Again, Mother Joachim sees none of the emotional responses one expects in someone who knows she is an object of affection. Sister Clare is coldly considering the problem.

"Despite the qualities we have seen," Sister Clare sighs, "we need to think long and hard about this. The man is a professional gunman. The man has killed."

"But the man also has the capacity to love, wouldn't you agree?"

Sister Clare again pauses a few minutes in reflective quiet.

"Well, yes." Sister Clare nods. "I do. I believe Ethan possesses a great capacity to love, and to love deeply."

CHAPTER 15

"So, you just going to wait?"

Leaning forward, Junior sips at his whiskey before responding. The two of them are alone at the bar. After leaving the bottle, Birnbaum, the owner and sole employee, excuses himself and disappears into the back room of the saloon. Junior eyes the speaker, one of his father's hired men who has become a friend of sorts. Always wearing a red bandanna, the man is agreeable and ready to perform the dirty chores for Junior that Rufe Harris expects his son to do. Most of the hands avoid Junior, but a few like the whiskey and idle hours spent with the boss's son.

"Maybe." Junior shrugs.

"Can't believe that so-called gunfighter let them get away with it."

"No one is getting away with anything," Junior sneers before throwing back the rest of his drink. "Hand me the bottle." After re-filling his glass, Junior turns and leans his back against the bar. "You listen up careful like."

"I'm with you, Junior."

"Few years back, my dad bought a filly for my sister, paid a lot of money, see? Well, I saddled this special little horse up when no one was around and sunk in my spurs to see what it could do. The damned thing bucked and spun and fought like hell. After I taught it who was boss, the damned thing bit me. Know what comes next?"

The cowhand with the bandanna shakes his head.

"Drew my pistol and blew its brains out, that's what!" Junior slaps the man's shoulder and laughs. "Put six in its pretty little head and made a mess of it."

"What'd Rufe do?"

"Mad as a hornet and my sister cried for weeks. She took off with my ma soon after. But ol' Rufe just grit his teeth and said nothing. So let that be your answer." Junior's eyes narrow and his lips peel back in an evil grin. "Nobody crosses Junior Harris and gets away with it. Nobody!"

CHAPTER 16

"Those clouds be getting ready to cut loose." Pickles spits a stream of juice for emphasis.

Two days of work have filled the rickyard, and now they are loading the leftover cuttings into the hayloft. Ethan estimates they will beat the storm, but it will be close. One more load should do it. Enough hay in the loft to feed three horses through the winter, with a fair amount left over. The Belgian will be well fed. Before leaving, he will inform Ba'cho about the surplus, just in case the winter proves harsher than expected.

"Hey, Ethan, don't forget I getsh to go shwimming."

"How could I forget? You remind me every hour like clockwork."

"Catch pneumonia, Jay." Pickles laughs. "But no one be swimming with this storm coming on."

Seeing Sister Clare again has made Ethan's dilemma worse. He hopes she will return before he leaves. He finds himself thinking about her all the time, wishing she was here, sharing in even the mundane things he does. He knows it is ridiculous. After all, they have only spent a few days together. But every time she returns, she is just as pretty and spirited and intelligent and strong as he remembers. Sister Clare is everything he thinks a woman should be. Even the thorns on her rose are attractive.

Gazing at the coming storm, Ethan finishes his thought. *Fight it all you want but you're in love with her. There it is. But should you be? Is it some type of sin? She has taken some sort of vows, but there has to be a way out if two people love each other. And that is the real question: does she have any inclination toward you, or are you just being a fool?*

CHAPTER 17

Of course Father Joseph is late in returning. Mother Joachim grinds her teeth. The demands on him are great, especially because his assistant is afraid to have an opinion about anything, let alone make a decision. Young Father Campos is as useful as a cup of spoiled milk. The decision will have to be made without the advice of the pastor. Besides, she knows what to do without the affirmation of the old Franciscan, who will undoubtedly agree with her anyway. Apache Jack, or Ethan, can be just as honorable and trustworthy as he appears. *But, as your instincts indicate, there is now another issue*, Mother Joachim thinks. *Sister Clare needs to be on guard.*

"Sister Scholastica, can you find Sister Clare and ask her to come see me at once?"

"Yes, Mother."

"No need to rehearse," Mother Joachim mutters. "Just tell her and observe her reaction."

"Mother Superior, Sister Clare is gone. Her overnight bag is missing and, when I checked the stable, the red mare and a saddle have been taken."

Mother Joachim slaps the table and stands.

"This note was left on her writing table."

"Read it."

"Mother, I observed the storm clouds gathering and waited for you as long as I deemed prudent. I shall return in three days with Jay if Ethan rejects our proposal. If he agrees, I will be back tomorrow, just as we planned. Yours in Christ, Sister Clare."

"Fool woman! It is *his* proposal I am worried about."

"Should I saddle a horse?"

"No, Sister." The Mother Superior manages a grim smile. "Those storm clouds are not threatening; they are unleashed. I only hope she makes it to the Morgan ranch before it catches her." A roll of thunder booms to emphasize her point.

"That was well timed, Mother."

"Yes, it was." Mother Joachim grins. "Besides, for whatever reason, I believe this is the way it is meant to happen. God be with them all."

CHAPTER 18

After arranging the slicker over the mare's rump, Sister Clare feels completely covered, except for the hood. That can wait until the rain actually starts to fall. Another glance at the sky confirms her expectation: those black clouds will overtake her soon, and when they do, the rains will come in torrents. Gathering the slicker's collar, Sister Clare fastens the clasp at her throat. Now she will be as dry as possible. Maybe she should have just waited for Mother Joachim to return. No, that would have delayed her another two days at the least. This storm will be a big one.

The wind suddenly increases, causing the trees to sway madly and branches to crack and fall across her path. A gust pushes her forward, causing her again to doubt her decision to race the storm. No, she must come now and not risk the chance Ethan will leave the moment the hay is in. For all anyone concerned knows, the work is completed and Ethan is long gone. Yet, that would be against everything the man seems to stand for.

What an odd situation. To think, they are trusting a gunman known as Apache Jack, a person with his past and reputation, with Jay's future. On its face it is absurd, yet considering all of the alternatives, it makes sense. The man is straightforward and appears to have a positive effect on people—except for those who violate his rather biblical moral code. Her reflections now confirm everything she, to her amazement, feels about the man: a great respect, if not a genuine liking of him! She must admit that her initial estimation of the man was wrong. Ethan possesses, in addition to his skills as a tracker and gunman, a sharp intuitive mind. He is an impressive individual and can be rather charming. Sister Clare giggles at the last thought. Yes, even Mother Superior admits being impressed by the man.

Sister Clare has taken his measure, as has Mother Joachim, and Ethan is not found wanting. Even when she told Mother Joachim the man's true identity, the Mother Superior confessed that not only was she already aware of it, but she knew far more of Ethan's history than Sister Clare did. It is a much more fascinating and violent history then she suspected, and yet Ethan never seems to deviate from his moral center. Even Ba'cho's clan, to a man, consider Ethan honorable and his word trustworthy. But would the man known as Apache Jack accept her proposition?

The rain begins to splatter around her, a wall of wet gray that envelops Sister Clare and barely gives her time to pull the hood over her head. She is approaching the series of meadows, each one larger than the next, which leads to the ranch. If she stays close to the tree line on her right, she should make it in another half hour. Keeping her head down, she resumes her thoughts. A crack of thunder causes her mount to whinny and rear. Unprepared for the sudden movement of the horse, Sister Clare falls backward over the rump and onto the earth. She sees a flash of lightening and then darkness.

CHAPTER 19

"No tasting," Ethan growls. "Just stir it."

"Shorry, Ethan." Jay hangs his head.

"It's all right, Jay." Ethan takes a breath and softens his voice. "When the stew is cooking, it's too hot to eat. It will burn your tongue. Won't be able to taste anything for days."

"I undershtand."

Staring out the window, Ethan shakes his head. *No, Jay doesn't understand, and it isn't his fault I'm cranky. What can have delayed her? If it were not for her, I'd have lit out for home days ago. You're a fool! You know nothing about women. Even Naki-Chaa laughs at you when you ask him about women. He has tried to explain how women are all the same but every one is different. What the hell does that mean? The Bible and Shakespeare are just as bad. Can you imagine trying to approach Sister Clare like Petruchio did Kate? You are a fool! But you can't spend the rest of your life wondering; you must find out.*

The door bursts open, and Pickles sticks his head in.

"Riders comin' on. Looks like them Injun fellers."

Grabbing his rifle and placing it next to the door where he can easily get to it, Ethan steps onto the porch. He tells Jay to stay inside and shuts the door. It takes a moment for his eyes to adjust to the darkness. The rain momentarily stops, which increases visibility. Ethan makes out five horses and four riders. Carlos is leading the group at a lope. Draped across the shoulders of Carlo's mount is a body.

The short hair and small hands belong to a woman. Ethan runs toward Carlos, knowing without seeing more who it is.

Carlos halts and lifts the limp form by her thick black belt. Swinging her headfirst toward Ethan, he drops her into his waiting arms. Ethan adjusts her to a face-up position and observes her breathing.

"Found her at small meadow where split tree stands," Carlos says, speaking in the White Mountain dialect.

"Can you come into the house and tell me?"

"For a moment." Carlos swings his leg over his horse's neck and drops to the earth. "We need to take the hunt back to camp before the rain returns."

Racing ahead, Pickles opens the door and nearly knocks an eavesdropping Jay over.

"Dang, boy, get out of the way and make yerself useful. Grab every towel and blanket you got and bring them to the stove."

Holding Sister Clare in front of the big wood stove, Ethan surveys the layout and makes his plans. She is already shivering, shaking more violently with every minute he delays. Thankfully, Pickles appears to be an old hand at emergencies. He clears the pot of stew from the stovetop and is gathering ropes and blankets.

"She did not fall, Cactus." Carlos stands just inside the shut door, obviously uncomfortable. "Her horse was shot. A graze across the rump."

"It threw her, then." Ethan nods. "Any other wounds?"

"The one on the horse. None on the woman, but we did not look close. Do you have medicine for the horse?"

"How bad?"

"Flesh."

"Not here."

"Then we will leave the saddle and take the horse with us."

"Thank you, Carlos."

Gently laying Sister Clare down, Ethan grabs a long rope and ties it to a post behind the stove. Without prompting, Pickles takes the coil from Ethan and follows along as Ethan makes a shoulder high square around the stove. Securing the rope as taut as possible, Ethan strings another rope along the floor. When this process is complete, they throw blankets over the top ropes, tying them to the bottom line, until they make a small room around the stove.

"Ish Shister going to be all right?"

"Hope so, Jay."

"You know she has to get out of those wet clothes," Pickles says quietly.

"I know," Ethan responds softly before continuing in a louder voice. "Jay, we need you to stack wood on the front porch."

"How much?"

"Bring ten loads from the barn."

"Okay! Come on, Kaisher, we're helping."

"And check for broken bones too. It's gotta be done Ethan."

All of the times you thought of holding her and kissing her and.... Ethan takes a deep breath and tells himself, *Just don't think about who it is!*

"Hand me the clothes and I'll hand you the towels." Pickles averts his eyes as he puts one foot through an opening between two of the blanket curtains.

"I'll need a few good wool blankets if you have any."

"These folks were sheep ranchers. Got nothin' but wool." Pickles chuckles nervously.

Don't look, Ethan tells himself as he unbuckles her belt and shoes. *No, that means you'll rely only on your hands and that will be worse. Act fast! Why do they need all of these layers? And could these buttons and clasps be any harder to undo?*

Flinging the wet garments to Pickles while gently flipping Sister Clare back and forth to get at the next article, Ethan is amazed at how soaked the clothes are. She must have been on the ground for a while. Lucky the horse stayed nearby; Carlos and his hunters may not have noticed her otherwise. As each layer of clothing is removed, Ethan checks for breaks and cuts and bruises. Finally she is naked. Grabbing the towels Ethan begins to dry off her skin. Her whole body is shivering. She is smaller framed than he supposed after days of observing her energy and physical strength. It is all the clothes she wears that make her appear bigger. Nothing broken, just some small cuts and nasty looking bruises, which are starting to color. *God, she's beautiful! Pretend she's a stranger you're helping out. Like the time you patched up the woman with the wound in her thigh back in Taos. Did Carlos or any of his men hear the gunshot? Why shoot at her? Towel off her head once more; short hair or not, it's still wet. There, good enough for now. Hope the storm leaves some signs of the ambush. That job will have to wait for tomorrow.*

"Pickles, where are the blankets?"

"Behind you."

Grabbing the top blanket Ethan lays it out and lifts Sister Clare onto it. He loosely rolls her into the blanket.

"Have one of the mattresses, Ethan."

Ethan steps out and helps the one-handed man carry the mattress into the makeshift room and places it next to the stove. Lifting Sister Clare onto the mattress, Ethan covers her with two more blankets.

"We need to stoke the fire."

"I'll get the boy to bring in some wood."

"Thanks, Pickles."

"You was nice and respectful Ethan. It had to be done."

Ethan nods.

"Nothing broke, I take it?"

"Some ugly bruising and small cuts on her, mostly the arms and legs."

"I'll get the wood. You be taking the first watch, I suppose."

"Yes."

CHAPTER 20

Ethan and Pickles share watch duties, keeping the fire hot and checking on Sister Clare's condition. During his second watch, Ethan returns from the front porch carrying an armful of wood and, using his foot, deftly closes the door behind him. Noticing one of the blanket curtains slightly open, Ethan uses that as his doorway to stoke the stove fire. Ethan immediately halts, his surprise quickly turning to wonder. He thinks knows a lot about horses and dogs, but the animals can still amaze him. Next to Sister Clare, his back snuggled against hers, is Kaiser. The shepherd's relaxed muscles and steady breathing mirror the now steady rise and fall of the young nun's chest. It is then Ethan knows Sister Clare will recover. Bending down to the dog, Ethan gently pats Kaiser's head. The dog opens his eyes and looks curiously at Ethan.

"Thank you," Ethan whispers.

The rest of the night Ethan keeps watch, alternately sipping coffee and checking on Sister Clare. It is during the pre-dawn glow of the eastern horizon that he wakes Pickles before slipping out to the barn to saddle his horse. Ethan then throws an old saddle on the suspicious Belgian. He needs to bring Kaiser along and that means Jay also, so he returns to the house. Ethan has just shaken Jay awake when he senses company. Opening the front door, Ethan smiles.

"Dagot'ee, Cactus."

"Thought you might show up."
"We should bring the wolf dog," Ba'cho responds.
"Agreed."

CHAPTER 21

It is a sound she knows, wood rhythmically creaking against wood. It is a rocking chair. Sister Clare purrs, thinking of all the fond memories that sound conjures up. Wiggling her toes, she pulls the blankets around her head, clasping the corners to her throat so that only her face is exposed. It is like those cold winter mornings of relaxing and snuggling when she was a girl. Father rocking in a favorite chair and smoking his pipe while Momma rolls out dough for one of those marvelous pastries. It is only when Sister Clare blinks through the crust of a long sleep and her eyes focus on the wood stove that she remembers the crack of thunder and flash of lightening. She recognizes the stove and knows immediately where she is. How did she get to the Morgan ranch? Did Ethan or Pickles bring her? She gasps, realizing that, except for the blankets, she is naked.

"That you, Sister Clare?"

The voice belongs to Pickles. Were they alone? *Dear God, I am naked! Who did this? Must fight this feeling of vulnerability. Calm down and think. Whatever has happened cannot be changed. Time to consider the present. You need information. It is awkward enough being physically unable to move, but you have to find out how you got into this condition. Why are you on the floor naked and wrapped in a cocoon of blankets? Who did this to you? You do not even know the date or time of day! Best to be calm and compliant until you can fill in the gaps and find out the reality of your circumstances.*

"I am awake," Sister Clare answers calmly.

"You had us worried, Sister. Thought you might get the chills and fever and that infloo-ensa."

"I feel fine."

"Can I get you some coffee or maybe some broth? Ethan thought a meat broth would help you. It's on the stove. Want me to fetch you a cup?"

"Perhaps later. Where is Ethan?"

"He and Ba'cho took off just after daylight to where you was ambushed. They wanted the dog to go too, thinkin' he might catch a scent or find a clue. Well, if you want the dog, you need to have Jay, so I appear to be the only one they didn't have any use for. Reckon you're stuck with me for company."

Turning to her right, Sister Clare feels an excruciating pain from her hip that returns her to her back. Her head throbs and a groan escapes her.

"Best move real ginger-like, Sister. Ethan said you got some bad bruising."

"You said ambush?"

"Yes, ma'am. Carlos and some others was returning to camp from a hunt, trying to beat the storm, and thought they heard two rifle shots. They investigated and saw your horse. Well, you was found all crumpled up nearby. Not much further away was your bag of spare clothes. The bag with your spare things was soaked too. So Carlos threw you over his horse and brought you here. Ethan set up this little room and dried you and rolled you up in those blankets. He knew what he was doin' all right, as good as most doctors I've seen. Nothing broke, just the bruises. I thought you were in big trouble, but he knew what to do." Pickles chuckles and adds, "So did that dog. Slept next to you all night and kept your back warm—the dog, I mean."

So it was Ethan who had removed her clothes and touched her body with his hands. The same hands that kill can also heal; they dried her and swaddled her in wool to save her. What a strange world this has become. Weeks ago she was so confident and righteous, but now she is reconsidering so much because of man she so quickly dismissed.

Staring at the ceiling, Sister Clare opens up a dialogue with her patron saint and confidant. How long has it been since she felt the need to do that? Amazing, she had laid helpless and naked before a man she had condemned before even meeting. What did he think while touching her? *No, he had one purpose and no other choice to save me. Had the roles been reversed, I hopefully would have the sense to do the same thing. Maybe, but even if I did, I would not have managed nearly as well. Yet, what did the man think while looking at and... best not to wonder. Ethan has been honorable thus far and acted from necessity. Good Lord, what a strange circumstance! All the debate about entrusting Jay's fate to Ethan, and now you are the one in the man's care.*

"Where are my clothes?"

"Look behind the stove on that makeshift clothesline."

She hears Pickles walk across the room and sees his one good hand touching her garments.

"Still damp, Sister. Not surprising given how soaked you was. Ethan was cursin' a bit at the amount of layers he had to peel off.... I mean no offense, uh, well.... Beggin' your pardon, but you see, he had to work fast so you wouldn't get the illness. You was shaking awful bad, Sister."

"Do you know who Ethan is?"

Footsteps are the only sound until they cease and the creaking of wood upon wood resumes. She hears movement as he settles in and, finally, the striking of a match. The aroma of pipe tobacco that fills the air, combined with the smell of wool and her own warm body odor, again reminds her of that youthful home, lying in bed at night while listening to her parents discuss matters great and small, Dad with his pipe and Momma with her knitting.

"I may not be as larnt as the rest, but, Sister, you are a better person than that. He did what he had to do, and no man could have been as respectful. I know of Apache Jack, and I knew he and Ethan was the same the moment Ethan lifted his head and I saw the scar under his chin."

"Scar?" The word escapes her lips before she can regain her balance. She is embarrassed at being admonished by Pickles of all people. Mother Joachim had never even mentioned the scar. Worse, Sister Clare hadn't noticed it.

"You didn't know?" Pickles chuckles. "Well, let me tell you how he got it, and maybe you'll larn some more you didn't know 'bout Mr. Ethan."

There is a pause while Pickles puffs to keep his pipe lit. She wants to respond in a cutting way to remind him of his place, but she is also quite curious. Why hadn't Mother Superior mentioned the scar? Sister Clare believes knowledge is always an asset, no matter how trivial or useless it might seem. Needing to know as much about Ethan as possible in making her proposal to the man, Sister Clare wonders what else Mother Superior has failed to disclose.

"I ran a livery down in Tucson. Had both my hands and was considered a top man with horses. Well, I heard the story from those who knew all three of the participants. There was this Injun who had been a scout for the Army. Well, he fell in love with this white gal, and they took to farming, growing fruit trees up in this high valley with a creek and little house and makin' a fine life of it. Well, a neighbor with too much cattle wanted the water from that creek. See, out here it's usually all 'bout the water. Well, these three desperado types on the run were hired by this rancher and came upon this happy place and killed the gal after... well, treating her rough and, well, then they tied up the Injun and drug him behind a horse. Unfortunate for them was this Injun was like Apache Jack's father. Now Jack came on the scene, and the three cowards recognized the horse and rider and skedaddled before he could get to 'em."

"How long ago?"

"Let's see, maybe eight? Yes, eight years ago be about right. About this time of year. Yes, it was right about the time folks be harvesting their crops. Got caught unawares, I suspect."

"Please continue."

"Yes, well, Jack is tending to the man when this Texas Ranger rides in. Seems he's been trackin' two of them that done a crime for killings back in Texas. Well, this ranger and Jack bury the woman and patch the man up so he can get by a few days, then they take after the desperados. A few days later they find 'em, only there was now five. Some unlucky men joined the wrong outfit. Apache Jack and the man from Texas left their horses a mile back and sneaked up and found the one on guard and slit his throat."

Sister Clare reflexively touches her throat. She can barely breathe as Pickles continues.

"Next up was the camp where the men were suppin'. Now they came up so they were behind all four of the bandits. About fifty, sixty feet from the camp, Jack and the Ranger stood up and walked toward the men. The lawman told them they were under arrest, and all four went for their guns. Jack and the Ranger kept walking forward, blazing away and dropping every one of them. The ranger took a bullet across his leg but nothing of a serious nature. One of the killers, a big man who had three bullets in him, was playing possum, and when Jack leaned over him, the killer tried to slice Jack. Got Jack under the chin before Jack put a bullet between his eyes."

"Pickles, I..."

"That's not the end, Sister. You see, after they buried these miserable men—nothing to mark the graves, since they didn't believe any of them deserved it—well, they sewed each other up, and the ranger took the outlaw gear back to Texas, and Jack went back and nursed his, well, father, I guess is the right word, back to health. The man was missing an eye, his nose and right cheek was scarred up, and he had a crippled leg that gave him a limp. Poor man didn't want to live, but Apache Jack would have none of it. From that time on, Naki-Chaa was no longer Apache Jack's teacher and dad, but his partner."

"What happened to the rancher?"

"Disappeared. No one knows for sure and no one asks, but seems there was a war party of Cibecue that rode nearby and may have taken the rancher into the mountains. Leastways, Jack had an alibi."

"And where is Naki-Chaa?"

"He's out west or up north, depends who you believe. He and Apache Jack took off a few years back, and when Jack returned, it was rumored they had bought a spread and covered their tracks so no one could find them. With a reputation like Apache Jack's, it would be a might more peaceful to have a new identity. Tell the truth, I'm surprised he came back. Must have been a job he couldn't pass on."

CHAPTER 22

The place where Sister Clare's horse was shot has been easy for Ethan and Ba'cho to find. Carlos and his men had walked and ridden over the area, but not enough to obscure the evidence. Carlos heard a shot and found the horse standing where Sister Clare fell. Her horse had reared at the pain of the bullet creasing across its back quarter, bucking the nun over its rump. All of this was discernible because Sister Clare's horse was the only one shod, so those tracks were distinguishable from Apache mounts. The wound on Sister Clare's horse indicates the shot had come from across the meadow.

The moment Ethan and Ba'cho start for the opposite side of the meadow, Kaiser races ahead and within minutes circles a spot behind a fallen tree. Two shell casings lay next to a small area of bent and crushed grass where the shooter had crouched. Three fresh cigarette butts show the man waited for no more than two hours the night of the ambush. But there is a pile of five or six older stubs nearby where the man had waited the previous day or two. They know it is a man because of the smokes and the boots and rowel marks. The boot prints indicated a short size, but the heel prints are deep. Kaiser growls and lowers into a crouch.

"Ethan." Jay's voice betrays his fear.

"There's no one left, Jay," Ethan assures as he follows the dog. "He found where the man staked his horse."

Kaiser circles a copse of aspens, slowly tightening the noose until he sprints into the trees. Ba'cho jogs in after the dog while Ethan holds back with Jay. Ba'cho pokes his head between the trees and motions for Ethan to come on. Ethan sees the horse droppings and cropped grass and stripped bark. The crisp, well-defined hoof prints indicate the horse has been newly shod. The ambusher hid his horse and waited to bushwhack Sister Clare.

"Good work, Kaiser." Ethan ruffles the dog's mane and pats him.

Walking back across the meadow, Ethan turns it all over in his mind. Why kill a nun? The entire territory would hunt a man down and lynch him for such a deed. *She comes riding along the edge of the trees. It's getting dark and starting to rain. She puts on the slicker and pulls the hood over her head. But she rides sidesaddle! Getting dark and she's covered up so she might be mistaken for a man. Who, then? Not you, nothing to gain, he* reasons. *If they knew who you were, they would have White Hair do it. Junior is a bully and bullies are cowards. People who lay in ambush either know the person is coming because they follow the person and jump ahead, or they know the person's routine. We faced off just after Sister Clare and Jay came back from town. That was just over two weeks ago.*

"Jay, do you ever go into town without the wagon?"

"Go to town? You meansh to shell the wood to Mother Joachim?"

"Yeah."

"Oh my gosh!" Jay slapped the side of his head in distress. "I forgot! I betsh that'sh why Shishter Clare came up here! I didn't mark the calendar she gave me. They need my wood!"

"It's all right. She told me she wanted you to wait until she came back."

"Really?"

Putting a reassuring arm around Jays' shoulders, Ethan gives the boy a friendly shake.

"You know how women are, always messing with our business."

"Meshin' with businesh! Yep, alwaysh meshin'."

"So do you ever go to town without the wagon?"

"Nope." Jay shakes his head.

If the shooter was after Jay, they would have known the rider was not him... unless the shooter never really studied Jay's routine. Someone who is rash and not prone to think things through. A person who often acts without considering.

Ba'cho trots up from where he has been examining the ground.

"The prints lead to the town. You know who this is?"

"Have a good idea. I can confirm it later."

"Why was he after the holy woman?"

"He wasn't."

Ba'cho glances at Jay, and Ethan nods in response.

CHAPTER 23

Blinking open her eyes, Sister Clare remembers her helpless condition. It is the sound of footsteps that wakes her up. Whoever is creeping in and working at the stove is trying to be quiet, and that condescending behavior irritates her. Knowing her response is irrational, even ridiculous, Sister Clare takes a few deep breaths to calm down. Despite the discomfort and pain from the bruises, she actually feels better. There has been so much to think about: the ambush, Jay Morgan, Rufe Harris, and her embarrassing circumstances. Time to get over the latter. Ethan's actions have, once again, been beyond reproach. Time to move beyond it as an unpleasant but trivial experience.

"Your clothes are dry, Sister Clare."

Slowly turning her head, Sister Clare sees Ethan. His back is to her as he places a pot onto the stove.

"I'll go with the others outside, and we'll stay in the barn until we hear you give us the all clear."

"Thank you."

Keeping his back to her, Ethan sidles through the curtains. Waiting for the door to close Sister Clare carefully sits up, allowing her head to clear. The smell of potatoes and carrots and onion and sage make her mouth water. She is starving, and even the aroma of coffee appeals to her appetite. While dressing, she sips some of the thick broth, sneaking a piece of meat and onion onto the spoon. The wool has kept her warm, but nothing beats the feel of food warming the body from the inside out. What had they used on her clothes? Obviously someone had attempted to launder her belongings, but with what cleaning agent? Very strange fragrance, if that word were even applicable. A hint of lavender and sage and baking soda and... good heavens, what else did they use? It gives the clothes a pleasantly wholesome odor.

When fully clothed and satisfied that she bears a resemblance to the nun who left the mission two days ago, Sister Clare removes the wall of blankets, folding them all and stacking them next to the loom. Next, she unties and unstrings the rope framework, standing atop a chair to reach the higher ropes. Finally, she arranges the furniture to its normal placement. Pleased that all appears as if nothing traumatic occurred, Sister Clare takes a deep calming breath and opens the front door.

There is no need to call them; the three men are standing in the barn door waiting. While cleaning, she had noticed the table set with cups and bowls and realized they were preparing to sit down for supper when she woke up. Jay manages a greeting before he and Kaiser bolt past her and straight for the table.

"Glad to see you back up and around, Sister." Pickles nods as he too makes his way to the food.

Ethan stops at the first step and touches the tip of his hat. Keeping his eyes fixed at her feet he loops his hands through the back of his belt and rocks from toe to flat foot. It suddenly dawns on Sister Clare that he doesn't know how to act. He is the one who is embarrassed!

"That goes for me also, Sister Clare." Ethan kicks at the wet wood. "You gave us a scare."

"I am better now." She decides to keep to her original plan and ignore his unclothing and touching her. "Did you discover who tried to shoot me?"

Ethan pauses. *Why is she so reluctant to acknowledge that we just spent two days caring and worrying about her?*

"Beg your pardon, Sister, but you were in bad shape. Even the dog knew enough to…"

"Yes, but now I am just fine. We have things to decide and do. Were you able to find out who it was who shot at me?"

"They were not shooting at you, Sister." Ethan looks up and their eyes meet. "They were after Jay."

"Jay?"

"He brings wood to the mission every two weeks or so? That's his job?" Ethan waits for a response, but Sister Clare just blinks, trying to process the information. "The shooter knew that and was expecting him. He had been there the day before, waiting. It was dark, raining, he saw a figure on a horse in a slicker with the hood up and took two shots."

"But who would want to harm Jay?"

"With Jay dead, no one needs him to sell. Unless you can produce an heir, this place would be sold at auction by the territorial government. Even if you brought in an aunt or uncle, they would be easier to negotiate with than you."

"But that's not what would happen." Sister Clare drops her shoulders in resignation. "You might as well know; Jay does not own this place. Before he died, his father deeded this ranch to the mission, with the provision that Jay be allowed to live here as long as he is alive. Jay has a life estate interest and no more in the land and buildings. The money from the sale of the sheep we hold in trust for him."

Processing the information, Ethan is incredulous. *These are intelligent women! Surely they can see how stupid such a thing is.*

"Do you understand the danger you've put this boy in?" Ethan does not try to temper the anger he feels. "Who else knows about this?"

"Don't you dare take that tone with me!"

"Someone ought to give you more than a tongue lashing! If what you say is true, there is no reason for anyone wanting this place to keep Jay alive."

"But the mission would never sell it!"

"Two years from now some bishop or other bureaucrat in your church is going to wonder why they own this ranch, and a cash offer will look mighty good. There will be some project or other mission that needs the money, and Rufe Harris will have made it clear he is a ready, willing, and able buyer. In fact, the way he has scared folks around here, he might be the only offer."

Sister Clare's mouth moves and her mind races, but no words come out.

"Think on that." Ethan keeps his voice even as he walks by her. "I'm hungry."

Feeling faint, Sister Clare hugs the porch post. A few remaining storm clouds lumber across the star-studded sky. Gazing up, she finds the little bear and constant Polaris. How has it all come this? Everything she and Mother Joachim so carefully planned and tried to control has gone awry. "Oh God," she murmurs, "despite all of our efforts, we failed in our task. Are we all really hostages to fate?"

CHAPTER 24

Nothing much is said between Ethan and Sister Clare the next day. It is agreed by all that Sister Clare needs another day to recuperate, but nothing else has been discussed. Pickles notices the tension between the two and hides out in the barn, finding and making up chores to keep out of the way. Jay notices nothing amiss and chatters to whoever will listen.

At day's end, the sunset creates a purple light in the trees and dyes the sky a rich orange, causing Ethan to pause and observe. He stands in front of the house, smiling at the show nature is putting on for him. Autumn days often end like this up in the mountains. It is these ordinary events that remind Ethan how wonderful life can be. He believes the smell of the grass after a rain or the sight of a calf kicking its feet with the joy of living should make a man stop and take notice, because they are important. If someone doesn't understand the miracle of just taking a breath, how can they appreciate life at all?

Stepping onto the porch from the house, Sister Clare notices Ethan staring into the distance. She can hear Pickles and Jay in the barn, rustling with livery and feeding the horses. She adjusts the shawl around her neck and shoulders. Even in the early fall, temperatures drop fast in the mountains when evening comes.

"I hope you will forgive me," she begins and notices Ethan flinch. He must have been deep in thought; she has startled him. It surprises her that she can surprise such a man. "I have been, as Mother Superior would describe it, 'arrogant in words and manner.' Pride is sinful, and I am sorry for the way I have thought and acted. You cared for me, and I didn't even thank you."

"You are strong willed, ma'am." Ethan smiles and leans against the hitching rail. "But I admire that trait in a woman. I don't think one can survive in this country without it. I think I could have checked my anger and maybe thought a bit before I spoke about Jay."

"I disagree, Ethan. I and everyone else missed the obvious with Jay. You shame me. From the beginning, I suspected you had a selfish motive, something to gain by helping Jay. You, however, are the only one of us who treats Jay well because it is natural for you. You're kind because you genuinely like him, not because it is the right thing to do or out of a duty to do so. We handled this without considering Jay's life. We looked at things from the wrong perspective."

"You give me too much credit. If you think about it, Ba'cho and his folks, Pickles, the Pebet family, and I suspect a lot of others are the same as me with Jay. You just need to realize we cannot really control most things. You more than anyone should know even the most powerful man doesn't have *that* kind of power."

"Strange that I was just considering that line of thought," Sister Clare sighs. "Regardless, I returned from the mission with a proposal for you."

As they speak and the air between them thaws and warms, Ethan becomes more convinced of his feelings. The way she says his name, the way she blushes and averts her eyes when embarrassed, those eyes as dark and inviting as the night sky—he loves all of it. But does she have similar feelings for him? Will he ever know unless he asks? Not now, but soon, if he is to ask at all.

Ethan is again staring into the heavens. Sister Clare decides to take a chance that he is off his guard and she can find out the piece of information she and Mother Superior desire to know.

"Where is Naki-Chaa?"

There is a pause, and Sister Clare tries to mask her disappointment. Apparently, Ethan is not so distracted that he can be fooled into disclosing the location of his ranch. The new home she is asking him to take Jay to.

"I promise there is a good reason for me knowing." Sister Clare's voice is earnest. "And I will keep it a secret."

"Let me hear your reason."

"Oh, very well, then. I will get to the point. The way things stand, Jay isn't safe. I came here on behalf of the mission to make you a proposal. We thought of hiring you to run this place, make it a working ranch again, and protect Jay."

"That is, or was, my line of work." Ethan smiles grimly. "I never thought the church would try to hire me. In this case, hiring me would start a war. Rufe Harris would hire every gunman he thinks is needed to kill me and give him an excuse to gun down Jay in the crossfire. I'm hiding up here to let my last job gather dust and allow every young hand wanting a reputation to forget about me."

"I understand that now. Our original plan was flawed."

"I'm sorry, but that plan won't wash. I can't keep him safe."

"Not here, you can't," Sister Clare agrees. "He might have a chance at the mission, but sooner or later, Harris is going to find a way."

"You can sell Harris the place."

"That is not an option. There is the promise we made to Frank Morgan, and if we give in to Rufe Harris, who will be left to stand up to him?" Sister Clare looks into Ethan's eyes and knows this is the right plan of action. "I am asking you to take Jay with you. If only for a year or two, until it's safe."

"A month ago, you didn't trust me."

"Reputations do not always give one a complete picture."

"Do you have one now?"

"No." Sister Clare laughs in spite of herself. Blushing, she readjusts her shawl. "Mother Joachim says I met my match trying to deal with you, and I must admit you are an enigma to me. How can you be hired to kill people and yet otherwise live with such strong Christian morals?"

"I never hired out to do violence, ma'am, but to solve problems. Those problems usually mean standing up to bullies. A real soldier never wants war, but the only way to prevent one is to make sure the other side knows you're prepared to go all in. The people I killed left me no choice."

"And now you are trying to escape it?"

"Kept most every dollar I earned. I've planned for this awhile. When I leave, no one will find me, and I will not return. So you still have no good reason to know where I'm heading."

"Will you take Jay?"

Through the lens of Ethan's feelings, he swears the starlight has gathered about her and sparkles in the darkness. He wants to pretend that she said "me" instead of "Jay." If she were not wearing the habit, it would be so simple. She is the best woman he has ever met. He wants her to walk with him through the rest of their lives together. Is this a good time to ask? Isn't it better to know one way or the other?

Sister Clare notices that Ethan is hesitating, maybe struggling to say something. He is looking directly at her, opening his mouth to speak but then dropping his eyes and lowering his head. He slaps the rail and gives her a quick, almost shy smile. Sister Clare wonders what has got into the man. He is acting like a young man afraid to ask a girl to dance. Finally, Ethan shakes his head, exhales, and turns away from her.

"You're the second person to ask me that. Let me sleep on it," Ethan comments quietly as he heads for the barn.

"Who was the other?" Sister Clare calls after him. She cannot imagine anyone else who might have considered this.

"Ba'cho."

"Ba'cho? Why?"

"I told you, there are a lot of folks out there trying to do what's right."

CHAPTER 25

Lying in front of Jay, Kaiser hears the boy and the one-handed man snoring, while their Alpha sits up, his back resting against a pile of hay. It is hard to tell if the Alpha is asleep. Unlike most men, he does everything quietly. Kaiser senses the anxiety in the Alpha and also in the woman. The Alpha's tension focuses inward, but the woman is nervous and confused. Getting up and slowly approaching the Alpha, Kaiser halts and sniffs at the man. The man raises his hand and scratches Kaiser's head, just behind the ear.

"It's all right, Kaiser," Ethan whispers. "I'll keep watch if you need to go someplace."

Walking to the partially open barn door, Kaiser pauses only a moment before going through and trotting toward the house. The woman is still up. He sees her pacing back and forth between the lamp and front window. Kaiser can smell something new and strong in her scent: fear.

Puzzling over it all evening, Sister Clare cannot pinpoint what has changed in her relationship with Ethan. Ever since she recovered, she senses the strong emotional currents flowing through the man—in how he speaks, his posture—something he is keeping pent up. Climbing into her woolen nightclothes, she reviews all of her interactions with him in the hope of discovering what is different. So much depends on him.

Adjusting her clothes, Sister Clare happens to see her reflection in the window and examines her face and body. Even with her hair cut, she might be considered pretty. *Good Lord, no!* Trying to fight down the panic, Sister Clare stares into the room, to the place on the floor where he undressed her. Approaching the spot where she had lain, she bends down and touches it. Sister Clare's breath becomes short as she imagines the scene. Calming herself, Sister Clare rises and steps back to the rocking chair.

Sitting in the rocker, Sister Clare recalls his every word and expression, every interaction between them, from the first moment they met until an hour ago. She then considers the change in Mother Joachim, Pickles, and even Ba'cho whenever Ethan is discussed or when one of them is present when she and Ethan have been together. All of them cautious, observant, expectant. Only one explanation fits.

Ethan is an intelligent man, a man of the West who has survived what would have destroyed others. He sees the world in black and white, right and wrong, and his greatest strength is that if he believes something is true, he will not be stopped. *The man is in love with me. That is the important matter Mother Superior wanted to discuss before I left. Ethan, Apache Jack, is in love with me.*

Rising, Sister Clare stops by the window to again observe her reflection.

Look at the self-righteous, focused, and determined defender of God and his church now! she thinks. *You have too many important matters on the grand stage to be concerned with the human beings in your life! You overlook the basic feelings and needs of the people you are supposed to serve, first with Jay and now with Ethan. Ethan is in love with you, and everyone sees and knows it but you.*

Placing a hand on either side of the windowsill, Sister Clare drops her head between outstretched arms. Staring at her bare feet, she remembers how as a little girl she loved the feel of the grass and the delight of careless play with other children. Then come thoughts of youth when she dreamed of boys and, later, when she wondered if young men thought her attractive. She recalls the tingling sensation and the rush of warmth in her body when a boy complimented her or attempted to court her in the shy awkward way of those new to their changing bodies. But she considered all of that and more when she made her vows. She found a more fulfilling love in the church. It is God who she fell in love with. It is service to God that fulfills her. And now, in the middle of her vocation, comes this strange man, possessing remarkable virtue yet capable of great violence, who loves her. How can this happen? She is a nun, committed to God, yet Ethan is in love with her! Apache Jack, the most remarkable man she has ever met. *Is this a temptation or reaffirmation? I must now face up to that question: how do I feel about him? Do I feel romantic love for him? Oh, dear God, please help me!*

A scratch at the door startles her. She backs toward the stove to grab a pot. The scratching persists and, with a quick realization of who it is, she runs and opens the door. Kaiser trots past her and lies on her bed.

"Even you know." She shuts the door and allows the tears to fall. "Oh, Kaiser!" She curls up next to the shepherd and puts an arm around him. "Just look at the mess I've made. What am I going to do?"

CHAPTER 26

It is a glorious spring morning. The previous night's clouds sprinkled just enough rain to wash the air clean and dampen the earth. The fruit buds are blinking open to the morning sun as the trees stretch their creaking branches awake. She loves this green land of river valleys and mountains, the ordered orchards and wild forests of oak and fir. It is a gentler land, so different from the high desert of the mission. Looking back, she sees the house with its big porch and the white swing Ethan built so she can sit in the shelter of the eaves when it is too hot to work in the summer or too rainy in the winter. Smiling, she wonders if the day will be warm enough to enjoy a cool cider after supper. Maybe she will bake the shortbread cookies he so loves. Stopping to breathe deep the sweet scent of the apple blossoms, she says a prayer of thanks for being so happy.

"So, there you are."

She heard him coming, his work boots negating the soft tread of his footsteps. His arms circle her waist, and he gently pulls her into his body. She feels his scratchy cheek nuzzle into her neck. No matter how hard he tries, he can never shave close enough for her. Patting his face, she begins to turn her head to him. He looks at her and begins to speak.

"I love you..."

I love you *who*? Who is Ethan speaking to? Is it Clare, or has she returned to her baptismal name? Which one is it?

Realizing she is kneading the fur on Kaiser's shoulder and nuzzling her face into his neck, Sister Clare rolls onto her back, staring at the ceiling. The big dog sighs, and Sister Clare smiles and pets the shepherd. The wood stove still glows, giving the room an orange hue while the furnishings cast long shadows on the floor and walls.

"I am sorry, Kaiser, it was a dream. Do you dream, dear friend? I have to make sense of my feelings."

How do I feel? Am I tempted by that life or not? Have I changed in my resolve or commitment? Am I betraying God? No, I would feel dirty and ashamed if that were the case. Ethan is, as strange as it may seem, the best man I have ever met. The real question, she thinks, *is whether Ethan and that type of life are more attractive to me than my work as a nun. I think I know the answer. Yes, I know the answer now. Good Lord, but I am tired.*

Emotionally drained, Sister Clare rolls to her side and snuggles her back against Kaiser. For a while she stares into the shadows and tries to think of a plan. One big yawn is followed by another, and—assisted by the steady rhythm of Kaiser's breathing—she finally drifts into a dreamless sleep.

CHAPTER 27

Sister Clare wakes up to the smell of bacon and coffee. At her first stirring, Kaiser rises and trots to the door. Sister Clare hears soft steps walking into the house. She knows it is Ethan. Only an Apache walks as quietly. His steps retreat to the stove and change to a shuffle as the ring of pot and pan on the stovetop indicate what he is doing. Sister Clare blinks her eyes open.

"Dogs often have a lot more sense than we do," Ethan comments after nervously coughing. "When Kaiser left last night, I had my suspicions on where he was going. I heard you open the door to let him in and knew you would be taken care of."

Did the man know what she had been through? The inflated balloon of self-worth had deflated and finally brought her back to earth! He might, and if so, did she have any credibility left? Ethan and Ba'cho and, she suspected, even Mother Superior must think her a comical strutting character, ordering everyone around like a princess. All of the time, the reality has been that she is an empress with no clothes. Sister Clare blushes at how appropriate the metaphor is. Summoning her courage, she sits up, wrapping a blanket around her torso. She is about to respond when Ethan continues.

"Before I finish cooking breakfast and get on with my own work, I'd like to say something, Clare, and I'd rather say it like this. That is, with you there and my back toward you. I don't think I could get it said were we face to face. Guess I am that cowardly." He pauses and sighs.

Oh no, she thinks. *I confess that you are the bravest and best man I know, but please don't say this right now.*

"I've spent all night trying to find the right way to approach this, so let me start by saying that I'll take Jay, no conditions."

"Oh my God," Clare whispers to herself as she blinks at the tears welling in her eyes. "You are so much better than I. I am not worthy of you. Please stop!"

"Second, I'd like.... No." His voice struggles with tortured words. "Clare, you are the finest woman I've ever known. I want you to come with us. You are intelligent, pretty, strong, caring—it all is a part of what makes you the most beautiful woman I ever met. I love you, Clare. I don't know if I am committing some sort of sin by saying these things, but going through life with you, ma'am, would be a most wonderful journey. I don't know if you feel the same way, but I'd like you to consider it."

She hears him take a breath. Clare grabs the corners of her blanket and pulls them tight to her throat.

"I know you are curious about my place. It is forty-five acres of fertile land. A small knoll near the back is where we are building the house. It will have a big porch to sit on and enjoy the evenings."

Oh, Ethan, she thinks, *I've seen it! I dreamed of it!*

"We are planting the land in orchards, mostly apples and plums, but we'll consider whatever else there might be a good market for. I suppose we'll keep a few chickens, but the fruit is our main focus. It's in a beautiful valley with a string of towns, all with fine squares in the middle where people gather and visit and celebrate. Just off the squares, there is usually a fine church with a school next door. I know we haven't had a courtship to speak of, but there is no other woman I'd consider marrying. If I need to ask permission from someone, well, let me know who, and I'll try to say it better than this."

She thought she was out of tears. Sister Clare watches as his shoulders sag with his ebbing hope that she will go with him. His voice borders on plaintive, but his pride keeps the proposal true to the man who is making it. Searching her memory, she cannot remember having such a raw emotional response, but she has never felt her heart break before now.

"I am going to check on the others and then head out to find Ba'cho and fetch your horse. I'll meet you all back at the mission. It will give you some time to think about my, well... my proposal." There is a pause and then a sigh. "I'll tell the boys you'll open the door when ready. Jay and I will need the wagon and Belgian when we head west. I hope you'll come, too."

The Apaches have hidden their tracks well. It takes Ethan all morning to find signs of unshod horses. As Ethan approaches a stand of trees trying to climb a series of granite crags, he hears a shout from behind and sees Ba'cho loping his horse toward him. Ethan waits. As Ba'cho approaches, Ethan sees the man has his left hand across his front, holding onto something. When he halts in front of Ethan, Ba'cho smiles and nods in greeting. Draped across the shoulders of his horse is a young dog, maybe three months old.

"He is the son of the wolf dog." Ba'cho cannot hide his pride. "The man Pebet gave him to me. He said a man with my name deserves to have pick of the wolf dog's children."

"You have chosen well."

Ba'cho beams with pride.

"Is the horse ready to travel?"

"To the mission, but not where you go."

"I am taking the boy."

"He will be safe with you and Naki-Chaa." Ba'cho squints at Ethan. "And the woman?"

"I do not know. I have asked her."

"She is strong, Cactus."

"I hope she comes."

"She would be a good wife for you. Let us get the horse."

CHAPTER 28

It takes longer than Sister Clare expects to collect and prepare herself to face anyone. She knows her face is still flushed and her eyes bloodshot because Pickles averts his look and Jay keeps asking if she is crying. Finally, the old man makes the boy pick up his plate and eat outside. By the time she ventures onto the porch, the wagon is loaded, the big horse hitched, and the barn closed up and ready for winter. Sister Clare doesn't bother to inspect the work. That is yet another lesson she has learned from her time with Ethan: to trust a man to work is to respect that he will do it right. If not, there will be consequences, but you give the man that first benefit of the doubt. She sits next to Pickles on the wagon bench with Jay running alongside.

"In another hour or so he'll get tired, and I prepared a place for him to nap back in the wagon bed." Pickles spits over the side of the wagon. "Should be a nice and quiet ride, Sister."

"Ethan is taking Jay with him."

"Right thing to do, Sister."

"He asked me to go with them."

"Figured that was coming, too."

"He is a better man than I would have ever thought. No, he is the best man I have ever met."

Pickles remains silent, not knowing exactly how to respond. He is surprised she brought the subject up. He knows she doesn't respect him much. Pickles stares straight ahead over the top of the horse, hoping the nun will say something, anything. *Good God, woman, do you want me to answer for you? I ain't got the callin', but if I was you I'd go! You got more will and courage than most men and are the most stubborn woman I ever met. Leave it to a man like Apache Jack to fall for a woman like you.*

"He is"—Pickles is careful with his words— "respected by folks I trust. The Apaches trust him. The rangers do, too, and they are a tough bunch to impress."

"Do you?"

"With my life."

The shepherd leads them all the way to the main road, through the town and into the mission. Kaiser passes through the gates and sits, panting, as they stop the wagon. Sister Clare startles Pickles by patting him on the knee and mouthing a silent "thank you." In the wagon bed, Jay remains sound asleep. Sister Clare steps down and walks to the Mother Superior's door. She knocks as a supplicant.

"Yes?" comes the curious response.

"Mother Superior, it is Sister Clare. I request an audience with you."

Mother Joachim sits back in her chair and makes the sign of the cross. It is not the voice of the self-confidant young nun, filled with righteousness, she has dealt with in the past. Something dramatic has occurred, and the woman she is about to see will not be the same woman who left here five days ago as Sister Clare. *Well, you are about to find out just how good of a Mother Superior you are.*

"Come in, Sister Clare."

Sister Clare sits down facing her, but no longer are the chin defiant and the eyes steely. The young woman is not beaten, but uncertain. Mother Joachim's first concern of some physical abuse and trauma appears to be unfounded. The woman across from her does not display any evidence of being victimized. This is an emotional and spiritual crisis, just what Mother Joachim tried to prevent. On her own, without any available counseling or advice, Sister Clare has discovered the man loves her. *The young woman's future life is at stake and you, Mother Joachim, are holding the keys to this particular kingdom. First rule: be honest. Second rule: it is Sister Clare's decision to make, not yours.*

"I wish we'd had a chance to talk before you left."

"It is better we did not." Sister Clare lets the tears well up. If they fall, so be it. "I had to find out this way. Before he told me he loves me, he shamed me. Not intentionally—I think he would be mortified if he knew that. He loves me so much, Mother, that it reminds me of Christ's love: unconditional." She pauses in an attempt to control her emotions. The floodgates are opened, but she cannot allow the dam to burst. "But we got what we wanted, Mother! Oh, yes, we found someone to solve our problem and take Jay off our hands and make us look like we really are doing God's work. When he found out about the ownership of the ranch, he saw it for what it is: a short-term solution that puts Jay in even greater danger."

Slamming her fists on the desk, Sister Clare stands up, glaring at Mother Joachim. With cheeks bright red and tears streaming down her face, the young nun clenches her teeth; her arms shake in frustration. The older nun barely manages to keep her composure. Mother Joachim understands that if the young nun has a breaking point, this is it. Slowly Sister Clare sits down, burying her face in her hands and sobbing. Sister Clare has weathered the storm. Mother Joachim remains quiet, giving the young nun time to regroup.

"I don't love him like that. I don't love him like that." Sister Clare takes a deep breath and buries her face in her hands. "But, oh my God, he deserves it!"

After calming her with long quiet embraces and two glasses of Father Joseph's best brandy, Mother Superior guides her young protégé to bed. She has heard it all. Through tears and confessions and self-reproaches, it has all come out. Yet, as she tucks Sister Clare in, Mother Superior is still not certain if the girl has made up her mind. *Dear Lord,* Mother Joachim prays as she raises her eyes to heaven, *you use the most amazing people to teach us. Apache Jack, one of the most feared men of the territory, not only a paladin of virtue but teaching Christ's love to the very people dedicated to serve you. This gunman has taken the moral high ground from us. Sister Clare humbled? Oh, I will make sure everyone at this mission understands. But now, what will she decide? Please, God, oh please, God, I pray you help her make the right choice!*

Mother Joachim spends the evening in conference with Father Joseph and Father Campos. The young priest sits uncomfortably, crossing and re-crossing his legs while wringing his hands. She almost asks him to leave. By the time Mother Joachim finishes her narrative, erring on the side of repeating herself rather than leave anything out, Father Joseph is smiling pleasantly.

"Well, that is quite a story," Father Joseph remarks softly. "But you are too hard on yourselves. Just because the problem isn't resolved the way you originally thought it should be, or is resolved by someone other than you, doesn't mean you failed. If we are providing Jay Morgan with the best life possible based on the means at our disposal, what does it matter if no credit is due to our efforts? We may have stumbled and bumbled in the process, but is the result a good one? Does it achieve our purpose?"

"Yes," Mother Joachim sighs, "but the man is a notorious gunman."

"And not half as bad as St. Augustine in his youth. As has been said, every saint has a past, and every sinner has a future. The only real difficulty we have left is Sister Clare. You are quite sure she was not violated."

"I was direct and firm in deposing Pickles." Mother Joachim nods confidently. "Ethan is beyond reproach."

Father Campos squirms and re-crosses his legs yet again as the older priest continues.

"Then the only question is, does she love him?"

"She has taken vows!"

"Yes, and life is full of detours on unexpected paths. This man sounds like a romantic: Shakespeare and 'right and wrong' and protecting the weaker man. Romantics are the worst because they are in love with the idea of being in love. I should know. I am shameless in my admiration of the love between a man and a woman. It is why I cry at weddings and baptisms. Could it be the fact she is a nun that is the attraction?"

"This is a love that developed from admiration and respect as well as the physical. I have witnessed them together. She is not 'forbidden fruit' or 'taboo'; she is a woman he wants to spend his life with."

Mother Joachim wants to get up and slap Father Campos. If ever a man was in silent hysterics, it is he.

"In this event, Mother, we must let Sister Clare decide."

"She says she doesn't love him as a wife should."

"That is today. Tomorrow is the important decision."

"Her vows?"

"Isn't that the lesson? There is only one ruler of all events. If God wants her to remain in the habit, she will. If God wants her to be a wife and mother, we must not stand in the way."

CHAPTER 29

As he nears the ranch, Ethan spends a moment to examine the ground. The wagon tracks tell the tale of their departure. It appears to have been mid-morning when they left. From the footprints, he can tell that Pickles drove the wagon, with Clare sitting next to him, Kaiser scouting ahead, and Jay trying to keep up. Ba'cho insisted on entertaining Ethan all afternoon before leaving with Sister Clare's horse in tow. Now it is too late in the day to attempt to reach the mission. It is an easy decision to spend one last night at the ranch. Ethan dismounts and unsaddles his mustang. After grooming the two horses and forking hay into their stalls, he strolls across the yard and enters the house. He can smell Clare as he walks in. He tries to imagine the sound of her voice.

You're a fool and you know it, Ethan thinks with a sigh. *She doesn't love me, and the entire mission is probably wondering if I am loco. But I still reckon it was worth a try, because she is the best woman I will ever meet.*

Ethan closes up the house and saunters to the barn, where he unrolls his blankets on a bed of straw. The rich gold of the evening darkens as he lies on his back, staring into his dream: He is working in his orchard and, looking up, sees her on the front porch waving at him. She is wearing a gingham dress and holds a cup of coffee for him. He takes off his hat and waves it back at her. She sets the cup down and beckons him to come. The smile she gives him moistens his eyes.

"My God, man, but you are the fool to think a woman like that would ever love you," Ethan whispers to the ceiling before closing his eyes.

Up and packed before dawn, Ethan checks the soundness of the two horses before setting out. Ba'cho and his men did a good job with the bullet wound on Clare's horse. Ethan's mount snorts at the delay; he is eager to be off.

"We have a long ways to go before we get to our new home," Ethan says, patting the horse's neck, "so save some of that energy."

Looking one last time at the Morgan ranch, Ethan shakes his head. He came up here to hide out and rest up. Instead, he has taken on a job for no pay, adopted a stray, and fallen in love. Life does have some strange twists and turns.

CHAPTER 30

Approaching her office, Mother Joachim is surprised to see Sister Clare sitting on the porch. Before mass, she told the young nun she wanted to meet with her after breakfast, but Sister Clare is never this prompt. Sister Clare has moved two chairs onto the porch and smiles as the Mother Superior ascends the steps.

"I hope you do not mind my moving your furniture," Sister Clare says as she waves a hand at the sky, "but it is such a beautiful morning! I saw a bird race across the yard, and even Kaiser let him pass without a chase."

Noticing the dog lying in front of the porch, Mother Joachim glances around for Jay.

"He's not up yet, Mother. Kaiser rises much earlier and often keeps me company in the morning. I never took the time to observe all the good things around me. I told you, didn't I, how Kaiser comforted me. I wonder how many times things like that happened and I never noticed."

Mother Joachim sits down next to Sister Clare and asks, "How are you feeling?"

"Like a burden has been lifted from my shoulders."

Good Lord, the Mother Superior thinks, *she has changed her mind. She is giving up her work to marry Ethan.* Mother Joachim is at a loss for words.

"You must have thought," Sister Clare continues, "that everything weighs so heavily on me, and every problem is a chore. But they are not and never really were, Mother. My work is a blessing. I chose this vocation because I *want* to serve. But to serve God is to serve with love. My attitude should be of joy and delight in my work and in dealing with others. Ethan showed me the way."

"Then you want to leave us?"

Sister Clare turns toward Mother Joachim and smiles sadly.

"No, Mother. I have always been committed to my work. Ethan taught me how to love it."

CHAPTER 31

It is posed as a question: does he want to go west with Ethan? Sister Clare, with the little knowledge she has, outlines the trip and the expectation that Jay will work the orchards and treat Ethan and Naki-Chaa as father and uncle. Of course, Kaiser will go with them, as will the Belgian and wagon. Mother Joachim tries to explain that Jay will probably never return, but he is so excited to live with his new idol that the discussion deteriorates into Jay shouting, "Oh, boy!" and popping up every ten seconds to look out the window for Ethan. Finally, they let him go watch from the front gate.

"Well, that went well." Mother Joachim chuckles sarcastically.

"He understands all that is necessary."

"You still believe we should not disclose Ethan's true identity?"

"I wouldn't know how to. Besides, if Ethan wants to start a new life, Jay is the last person to trust with a secret."

Waiting at the gate lasts an hour. Jay begins to ask everyone he can the time and if they have seen Ethan. When he sees Pickles carrying a box of tools to the stables, he runs over and asks where Ethan is.

"It's about a half day's ride from the high meadows, Jay, you know that. Why don't you make yourself useful and help me out?"

"I got to wait for Ethan. Ish he coming down through the town?"

"That's the route."

"Oh, boy!"

"Now, why don't you wait in here and help me out?"

It is no use. Too excited, Jay runs on the road toward the town. If Ethan is coming on the trail from the meadows, Jay can go through town and meet him. Catching sight of the smithy and warehouse at the edge of town, Jay slows to a walk. He does not want to be out of breath when he finds Ethan. "Like a new pa," they had said. *Oh, boy!*

Kaiser has been in his usual position, running ahead of Jay, scouting. Suddenly the dog halts, hackles up, and then sprints back to Jay. The shepherd tries to turn Jay, even nipping at his legs as the boy tries to bull forward.

"Hey, Kaisher! Shtop! What'sh wrong with you?"

The big dog leans into Jay, pushing him to the southern side of the road.

"Thought that was you and your dog." Junior Harris emerges from the shadows of the warehouse. He is flanked by two of his father's cowhands.

Wheeling to face the men, Kaiser lowers into a crouch, growling.

"Haven't forgot that me and your dog have unfinished business, did ya, half-wit?"

The two cowhands spread out to either side of Junior. Kaiser eyes both of them but keeps his focus on Junior. The three men stop about forty feet away from Kaiser. Now aware of danger, Jay begins to back away.

"You leave ush alone," Jay pleads.

"Payback!" Junior shouts.

All three men draw their handguns and fire. The moment the men move their hands Kaiser lunges forward. The big dog comes within ten feet of Junior when a third bullet puts him to the ground. Kaiser hears Jay crying as a fourth bullet strikes and he exhales a last breath.

"No!" Jay cries over and over until he reaches Kaiser. Hugging the dog's head his cries became sobs, and he buries his face into Kaiser's mane.

"Told you, stupid. No one messes with Junior Harris."

CHAPTER 32

The sun is at Ethan's back when he finally turns onto the main road. He previously scouted the little town of approximately two dozen buildings and is now curious to actually ride through it. The saloon has four horses hitched in the front. Ethan recognizes Junior Harris's pinto in between two others. The fourth horse is tied to a different rail. So Junior and two friends are together; the other is probably a drifter. The dry goods store looks empty. In fact, the town is quiet for midday and appears almost deserted. As he nears the far side, he sees a warehouse with the Harris name proudly displayed in red paint across the front. After he passes, he notices the dirt in the road ahead has seen quite a bit of action. Wheel marks from a wagon that has turned down the road away from town. There is fresh blood by the wagon tracks. Scanning the surrounding ground, Ethan sees the spent casings. Alongside the wagon tracks is another set of hoof prints. Shod, powerful, but not a horse—a mule.

"Okay, we ride," Ethan mutters as he gradually accelerates the two horses into a gallop.

The mission comes into view, and Ethan swings into the courtyard. The wagon is in the middle of the courtyard with a crowd of people surrounding it. The group of people in and around the wagon bed consists of priests and nuns, along with Pickles and a large man in a leather apron worn by blacksmiths. There is only one person missing. Ethan dismounts and strides to the wagon. Jay is sobbing inconsolably as he sits in the wagon bed. A young priest turns to confront Ethan.

"Who—?"

Ethan shoves him aside and steps onto the wagon bed. Jay is sitting with Kaiser's head on his lap. The shepherd's lifeless eyes stare and his sagging tongue droops ignominiously as the gaping humans looked on.

"Who did this?"

"It was Junior," Pickles responds. "The smithy and his wife heard gunfire, and they saw Junior and two of his cronies kill him."

"My wife stayed with the boy and dog while I hightailed it down here," the smithy adds.

Ethan lifts Kaiser's body and steps down from the wagon. He finds Pickles, looks him in the eyes, and commands, "Show me the graveyard."

Motioning with his stump, Pickles ambulates across the courtyard followed by Ethan carrying Kaiser. Mother Joachim and Sister Clare lean into the wagon bed and grab Jay's arms. Guiding him out of the wagon, they follow Ethan.

"Father Joseph," Father Campos says in alarm, "I think he is going to bury a dog in the cemetery!"

The remaining nuns and Father Campos glance expectantly at Father Joseph.

"Then we should help him bury our lost friend," Father Joseph calmly responds.

Gathering a pick and two shovels from the stall where the tools are kept, Father Joseph places them on his shoulder and marches to the graveyard on the far side of the church. The old priest has never felt so confident that God's hand is directing every event. It is the first time he has seen the man called Apache Jack, but after all he has heard, he now knows this is a special man. If he possessed the man's presence, he would be a bishop. Praying that God will guide his words and acts, Father Joseph prepares to meet the man who is about to change the mission for years to come.

"Here." Father Joseph indicates a sight next to the church. "This is where those who have served the mission are interred. It is a place where a noble creature of God should lie in honor."

Placing a shovel and pick on the ground, Father Joseph begins to dig. Gently laying Kaiser's body down, Ethan removes his vest and gun belt and selects the pick. Pickles reaches for the remaining shovel, but Sister Clare pulls him away and takes up the spade. The three dig in silence. Occasionally, Ethan and Sister Clare's eyes meet, each trying to read the thoughts and emotions of the other.

As expected, Sister Clare observes the calm determination in Ethan that masks a building outrage. She understands that he will coldly channel his emotions into violence. She hears a dirge of death with each strike of his pick. The man will exact vengeance and, like a terrible flood rushing down a canyon, there will be no stopping it. But she will try.

The hole has to be deep to keep scavengers from violating the body, and Ethan drives the workers on by example until he is satisfied. Father Joseph is exhausted, and Sister Clare works until her blisters are smearing the handle with blood. Mother Joachim and Pickles step in and finish for her.

"That's enough," Ethan says as he jumps into the grave.

Father Joseph lifts Kaiser and hands him to Ethan. Ethan feels the rigor setting into the body. Gently arranging Kaiser into a prone position, like he is resting his head on his front paws, Ethan lifts himself up. Taking a shovel in hand Ethan, with the help of Pickles, quickly fills in the grave. As he tamps the top dirt down, leveling it with the surrounding earth, he feels a hand on his shoulder. It is the old priest with Jay at his side.

"Saint Francis," Father Joseph intones, "you are known for interceding on behalf of certain animals. We ask you to intercede on behalf of this great dog, Kaiser, as noble a creature as has walked with us here on earth and deserving of your intercession and blessing. Amen."

As they turn, Father Joseph sees the younger priest staring at him.

"We will plant a rosebush to mark the grave," the elder cleric announces. "That will be your task, Father Campos."

Looking around to locate Sister Clare, Ethan notices she is gone. He immediately glances to where he left his things and sees the gun belt is missing. Grabbing his vest, Ethan strides to the courtyard, eyes searching every door and window and shadow. He sees no movement. He starts for the office, then pauses, turns ninety degrees, and approaches the chapel. That is where she will choose to confront him—on her ground.

Shutting his eyes as he pushes through the church doors, Ethan re-opens them in the dim candlelit room, his eyesight quickly adjusting. She is kneeling in a pew, facing the altar. As he walks up the center aisle, Sister Clare makes the sign of the cross and steps out from the pew to face him. Her hands bear the sores and dried blood from her work in the graveyard. Her face is streaked with the sweat and dirt from her labors. Directly behind her is the crucifix with the figure of the Christ making the ultimate sacrifice. Ethan thinks it an appropriate setting.

"Hello, Ethan."

"Hello, Clare."

Looking at her, Ethan sees in her eyes, in her face, and in her posture that she loves him. But it is a love of respect, not of romance.

"I hid your guns, Ethan. Jay told me after your last job you kept only one handgun and a rifle because you did not think you would need them again."

"I was wrong."

"Jay also heard you tell Ba'cho you would do anything for me."

"Jay keeps no secrets."

"I thought about bargaining with you, of agreeing to go with you and be your wife if you would not kill Junior Harris. As I prayed, I understood how you would detest such a proposal and how it would demean me in your eyes. I could not bear that, Ethan. With all of your sins, I think you are the finest man I have ever met. For the rest of my life, I shall measure everyone against you, and they shall be found wanting."

"I guess I will have to accept that and let the other go." Ethan steps forward and, taking both of her hands in his, kisses them. "I hope God will forgive me if I fell in love with one of His most beautiful creations."

"Thank you." In spite of herself, Sister Clare blushes. She squeezes his hands and says, "I have been praying for some way to stop you, but this isn't it. You live by a code I now understand but cannot accept. There has to be another way!"

"When an animal goes mad, there is no other way but to kill it."

"Is there anything I can say that will make you turn away from this?"

"These men chose their path, and if I don't put an end to it, they will get worse and they will get stronger. They tried to kill you, and they killed Kaiser. I am the consequence they will face."

"Your weapons are next to the altar, behind the statue of St. Joseph."

Ethan strides forward and straps on his gun belt. After checking the cylinder to make sure it is fully loaded, Ethan twirls the pistol into his holster. Despite the days of haying and hard labor, his fingers are nimble enough to get the job done. Ethan makes two practice draws and all feels right. Picking up his rifle, he starts to leave.

Observing his determined expression and lethal gun handling, Sister Clare closes her eyes in resignation. Then, as she hears him lift up the rifle, she draws a breath and faces him.

"While you are here, I want you to look up at the figure of Christ."

Ethan complies.

"Please, Ethan, consider his sacrifice to save you."

"Believe me, ma'am, I do a lot of thinking on that. He reconciled man and God at the cost of his life. I stand between folks like you and men like Junior Harris. I think God understands."

"I pray someday God grants you peace."

"Thank you, Sister Clare."

CHAPTER 33

White Hair sits in the shadows of the warehouse, smoking and contemplating quitting the job. It has been dull and unchallenging. The only excitement was with the hired hand at the Morgan ranch. Rufe might think the man unremarkable, but he handled that rifle like he knew his business. Now that crazy son of his has not only mistakenly ambushed a nun but killed the boy's dog. He is up at the saloon now, bragging on it like he is the next big pistolero. Time to move on. Six months' pay for no action. Drawing on his smoke, his eyes widen and he sits upright. *Well, well, things may have just changed!* He pauses to see what direction the horse and rider are heading before walking back to the office to find Rufe. The elder Harris sits behind his desk, working on his ledgers.

"Mr. Harris," White Hair drawls, "Morgan's hired man you didn't think so much of? He's heading up to the saloon, and he's packing a gun."

CHAPTER 34

Birnbaum's Saloon is owned and operated by a man who enjoys company but not relationships. He provides alcohol and tobacco products to the men who come into his establishment and couldn't care less if a woman ever enters through the saloon doors. He never says much but encourages the use of his establishment as a meeting place for the locals. He regards the merits and recognizes the foibles of the populace and welcomes all. Of late, however, he has noticed a drop off in his clients and profits, and he knows why. Ever since Rufe Harris decided he wanted to be the big stud of the high country, his son, already obnoxious, has taken the next step and become an insufferable bully. All too frequently Junior Harris and his toadies enter, order a bottle of whiskey, and stand at the bar, making sure their exploits are told loudly enough for all to hear. Everyone but Junior knows that his threats carry little weight. It is the shadow of the white-haired gunman Rufe Harris hired that stands behind Junior's boasts. So no one stands up to Junior, and no one challenges Rufe. The town is intimidated, and Mr. Birnbaum is fed up. At least the ranchers are not cowed—not yet, anyway.

John Pebet and Bill Smithson sit sipping beer by the wood stove. The two small ranchers are discussing their hay yields and the coming winter. Near them sits a cowboy nursing a shot of rye. The cowboy had drifted into the town looking for work. He asked Birnbaum about prospects, and the saloon owner liked the man's cut, so he advised him the opportunities might be better around Prescott and warned him against the Harris outfit.

On this day, the atmosphere at Birnbaum's had been congenial until Junior Harris burst through the doors with two of his father's hired hands in tow. After ordering a bottle and proceeding to swill the liquor and slap each other on the backs, they begin to loudly brag about killing a mad dog. Birnbaum and the ranchers try to ignore Junior while the drifting cowboy eyes the scene curiously.

"...and the moron blubbered, 'I wilsh gesh yoush.'" Junior beats the bar counter and laughs hysterically.

Birnbaum's eyes widen as he realizes. *My God, they are talking about Jay Morgan! Oh my God, no—they killed Kaiser!* He glances at Pebet and Smithson. They too sit staring at each other with wide eyes as the awful story comes out of Junior Harris's mouth. What will the sisters at the mission do? What can any of them do? The cowboy observes the reactions of the barman and ranchers and gradually pushes his chair back to face the room. At the moment Pebet's, Smithson's, and Birnbaum's eyes meet, the front swinging doors of the saloon are pushed open.

Taking three steps into the room, Ethan has the layout. Long bar in front of him, on the right of which are Junior and his two men. To the left is a wood stove and John Pebet sitting across from another man at a nearby table. Near the front window, to Ethan's immediate left, sits a cowboy, facing the room and anticipating trouble. The cowboy nods slightly and tips his hat in greeting. Ethan doesn't recognize the cowboy, but the man obviously knows him. From the man's gear, he looks to be drifting, looking for ranch work. The man has none of the signs of a gunman, but Ethan senses he has at least seen his share of fighting. Military? Lawman? While the man might be more than he appears,

Ethan recognizes the posture of an observer, not a participant, in the coming action. To Ethan's right, the tables are empty.

Junior and his friends are laughing so hard that they do not notice how quiet the room has become. Junior glances at Birnbaum and follows the storekeeper's gaze.

"Well, looky here." Junior laughs and slaps the shoulder of the cowhand on his right. "This is my lucky day! I get to settle two scores, boys. This is the half-wit's hired hand. How low can that be?"

Junior and his men all chuckle, but one of the men looks nervous.

They don't know who he is, the drifter at the table thinks, making sure he is out of the line of fire. *These fools are preparing to draw on Apache Jack!*

"A few days back, you ambushed someone you thought was Jay," Ethan says softly while staring at Junior, "and now you killed the boy's dog."

"You can't prove I was the one who shot at that nun."

"Could have even before you just admitted it, Junior. You see, no one outside the mission and the Apaches knew about it. No one else knew it was one of the sisters. No, Junior, I had enough evidence before you just now confessed to it."

Junior blinks, confused. He shakes off his thoughts.

"So, what are you going to do about it?"

"Depends on you. Drop your belt, and I'll take you down to the Presidio and let the Federal Marshal charge you."

"That will never happen!" Junior smirks.

"I figured that. You pull, and I'll finish the job."

"All three of us?"

"It took three of you to kill an animal that was worth more than all of you put together." Ethan notices how they are standing shoulder to shoulder. They all carry their guns to the right; only the one to his left has a clear draw. "I figure I'm more than enough to kill three men worth less than one dog."

Junior's lips curl in anger before he draws; his two henchmen are a second behind. Ethan fires once at Junior and fans two more at the man with a clear draw. The first shot hits Junior in the left shoulder but the second two are dead center in the breast of the man to Junior's right. Ethan observes that the man on Junior's left, wearing a red bandanna, is struggling to clear his weapon, so while firing his first three shots, Ethan steps forward and to his right to force the man to shoot across his body. Ethan also wants to draw fire away from the other men in the saloon. The man wearing the bandanna curses as Junior falls into him. Just as the man pushes away from Junior, Ethan takes a shot that misses. The man wearing the bandanna shoots wide as Ethan quickens his rightward movement. Suddenly Ethan kneels and fires twice just as the man with the bandanna shoots again. Ethan's first bullet is a gut shot that bends the man over. Ethan's second strikes the man in the neck. As he stands up, Ethan notices the man's second shot has hit the post next to him. A few of the wood splinters are stuck in his vest.

Walking forward, Ethan sees that both of Junior's henchmen are on the ground, staring eyes glazing over in death. Junior is writhing on the ground and wailing like a banshee.

"Help me! I'm shot! Oh, why won't someone help me?"

Ethan watches as Junior scoots and squirms across the floor until he pushes himself into a half sitting position against a wall. Emptying the spent casings, Ethan reaches back to his belt and grabs two bullets. The screams drown out the footsteps rushing up the steps and across the porch, but not the doors swinging open. Ethan turns in time to see White Hair's two pistols pointing at him. Rufe Harris stands next to his hired gun.

"I want to be the one to kill you for this!" Rufe snarls and begins to pull his gun.

"Everyone remain real still."

The commanding voice causes every head in the room to turn toward the drifter. The stranger has his handgun pointed at White Hair.

"The man has an empty gun, meaning he's basically unarmed. He let those three pull first. It was a fair fight. I know you'd want the same." The drifter nods toward White Hair.

Smiling, White Hair holsters his guns.

"What are you doing?" Rufe growls.

"Professional courtesy." White Hair calmly looks at Rufe. "Didn't you hear the man? He's unarmed. Besides, even though your son isn't very good, the man took down all three. And the bartender has a shotgun on us."

During the shooting, Birnbaum saw the drifter slowly pull out his gun and rest it on his lap. At the same time. the bar owner reached under the counter and took out his sawed-off shotgun. Until the drifter leveled his gun at the white-haired gunman, Birnbaum was unsure which direction to aim; now he knows.

"That's right, Rufe," Birnbaum says from behind the bar, "and I'll use it. Junior tried to kill one of the sisters, and he did kill Jay Morgan's dog. He has it coming."

"Load it, mister," White Hair tells Ethan.

Calmly and deliberately, Ethan faces his two antagonists while filling all six chambers. He twirls his gun into his holster, not to show off but to make sure it still feels comfortable and balanced in his hand. He sees White Hair watching him curiously.

"I am called Apache Jack," Ethan announces to White Hair. "I figure a man should know who is about to kill him."

Rufe Harris's eyes grow wide. White Hair's eyes narrow.

"You haven't crossed me," Ethan tells the gunman. "You can step out if you want."

"I took a contract," White Hair confidently replies. "Besides, I have a reputation to build up."

"It ends here."

"Prove it."

The two gunmen draw at the same time. White Hair is fast on the draw, but Ethan a split second faster, and that is the difference. Ethan ignores Rufe, who is just reaching for his gun after Ethan and White Hair have cleared leather. Ethan fires two shots at White Hair, both striking the torso. Just at the moment the first bullet hits him, White Hair gets off a shot. The force of Ethan's first bullet alters White Hair's aim enough that his shot only grazes Ethan's ribs. The three shots are barely discernible, but the staggering form of the white-haired gunman makes it obvious he is the recipient of two of them. The second shot from Ethan buckles White Hair's knees, causing the gunman to pause briefly before falling backward through the swinging doors.

Although he feels the sting of the wound, Ethan turns to the big rancher and buries three bullets into Rufe before a return shot is fired into the floor. Rufe tries to raise his weapon, but his arm slowly lowers and his weapon harmlessly clatters at his feet. As the big man stumbles toward Ethan, he shakes his head in disbelief. Coughing blood, Rufe looks at Ethan and mutters, "Apache Jack." The rancher is dead before his head hits the wooden floor.

Ethan hears the scuff of a chair and the drifter shouting, "Get down!"

Dropping to the floor, Ethan hears the sound of two pistol shots in rapid succession along with the thunderous boom of a shotgun. In seconds, the room becomes deadly quiet. Ethan remains still, listening to the footsteps of boots and the jangle of spurs. The drifter walks by Ethan and out the door to White Hair. Lying on the floor, too tired to get up, Ethan watches the drifter bend over White Hair for a moment before walking back into the saloon. The man acts with authority, certainly not like a drifting cowboy. The drifter comes toward Ethan and crouches next to him.

"You okay, Jack?"

Only a lawman would act with such confidence and address him as "Jack." Although he has never met him, Ethan recognizes the man as a ranger.

"I think he got me on the side."

"Let's take a look." The ranger rolls Ethan over. "More damage to the shirt and vest than you."

"What was the firing all about?"

"That Junior fellow decided to take a shot at your back. Not much left of him after both barrels of the shotgun. Doubt if you could find where my two bullets hit him."

"Thanks."

"You can thank Birnbaum, too. My name's Bob Vega, Texas Ranger." He offers Ethan a hand up. "Came here on the trail of that fella," he adds, nodding toward White Hair.

"Who is he?"

"Name of Zach Luckey. He accidentally shot a ten-year-old boy during a gunfight and is charged with manslaughter. Was trying to figure how to take him when you showed up."

"Seems like every time I'm with you rangers, I get hurt." Ethan grins. "Folks around here call me Ethan."

"Fair enough. I will need your statement for my report. Where you staying?"

"The mission down the road."

Bob Vega raises his eyebrows in surprise.

"It's a long story, Bob. By the way, I'd like to move on in the next few days."

"I'll be down to see you tomorrow. Rumor is that you had finished your last job and was leaving the territory."

"It is true. This here was unexpected. Can I fill you in tomorrow?"

"Sure thing. And, Ethan, most of us rangers will be sorry to see you go."

"Sure thing. And, Ethan, most of us rangers will be sorry to see you go."

CHAPTER 35

Word of the "Birnbaum Shootout" quickly spreads. The saloon owner, seeing a business opportunity, becomes occupied with plans of expansion, updating his signage and reconfiguring the interior to mark the positions of each participant. The small ranchers and townspeople, while not celebratory, engage in a collective sigh of relief. The threat of conflict and intimidation by the Harris ranch is gone. People now feel at peace to go on with the business of life.

Bob Vega, Texas Ranger, finds the backstory to his investigation more interesting than his pursuit of Zach Luckey. Visiting the Morgan ranch and interviewing Ba'cho and his brother give him a good background. Sister Clare and Mother Joachim, guarded in their disclosures, did not count on the handyman opening up and filling in their testimony over beers at Birnbaum's Saloon. Even so, it is Jay Morgan, the center of the whole story, who indirectly fills in the motives of all concerned. It is quite a tale. The ranger decides to include it all in his report.

Father Joseph, de facto doctor at the mission, tends Ethan's wound. The scent of the balm has the same curious odor of the one the Apaches use for their horses. The priest proves to be a good physician, and Ethan is ready to leave the day after he gives Bob Vega his statement.

Sister Clare visits him just after Father Joseph finishes tending his wounds. Ethan, resting on his hospital bed, recognizes Clare's footsteps as she enters the narrow infirmary. He wonders how she will act. It is awkward being here with everyone at the mission knowing what happened between them. Stopping next to his bed, she takes his hand and smiles down at him. He imprints her smile in his memory, so sweet it almost stops his breath.

"Hello, Sister." Ethan returns her smile.

"Before I took my vows, my name was Miriam."

"A right pretty name that suits you. But I will always remember you as Clare."

Sister Clare smiles and squeezes Ethan's hand.

"I'm leaving to open our mission school. Mother Joachim says you recommended that I be the headmistress."

"There is really no other choice. You will do well."

Leaning forward, Sister Clare gently kisses his forehead.

"Goodbye, Ethan," Sister Clare whispers, "and thank you. I am such a better person having known you." Straightening, Sister Clare raises Ethan's hand and kisses it. "I will never forget you, Ethan. I will pray for your happiness."

"You take care, Sister."

The mission is converting the Morgan ranch into a school for Ba'cho's people. Ethan suggested the idea as a way to provide some stability for Ba'cho's clan, and it was embraced and expanded on by Father Joseph and Mother Joachim. Sister Clare is put in charge, an appointment that everyone knows to be the right choice. Sister Marie is to assist her.

Two days after the gunfight, Ethan and Mother Joachim go through Jay's belongings and discuss whether any of the furniture at the cabin is wanted. Jay spends much of his time decorating Kaiser's gravesite and helping water the rosebush he and Father Campos have planted. Finally, on the morning of departure, the wagon is packed, and the sisters send them off with enough provisions for a month. As the sun reddens the eastern sky, Ethan and Jay say goodbye to Kaiser and climb onto the wagon. Father Joseph, Pickles, and Mother Joachim are there to see them off.

"May God bless you with a peaceful life filled with joy," Father Joseph says, shaking Ethan's hand.

"Thank you, Padre."

Mother Joachim kisses Jay on the cheek and dabs at the tears in her eyes. Walking around to Ethan, the Mother Superior grabs his hand and holds it in hers.

"There is someone out there for you, Ethan," Mother Joachim avers, "and I know you will experience the love you deserve. Believe that, my son!"

"Thank you, Mother Joachim."

"Let 'er buck." Pickles pats the Belgian's shoulder and moves aside as the wagon heads out the gate with Ethan's horse in tow.

As the wagon turns the corner and heads west, Ethan sees Ba'cho and his brother. The two men pull their mounts alongside the buckboard.

"Sister Clare told us you were the one who said Morgan's ranch should be used as a school for my people."

"She talks too much."

"She is working there now with another sister. We will help."

"Thanks."

"I have a gift for you, Cactus." Ba'cho holds out Kaiser's puppy. "The boy will think it is for him, but it must be yours."

Ethan knows how much Ba'cho wants the dog, but he cannot insult the man. Besides, if he is anything like his father, the dog will be a great addition to his place.

"You honor me, Ba'cho."

"Do not worry, Cactus. Pebet has another son of the wolf dog almost as good as this one."

Ethan hands the pup to Jay.

"Recognize him? He's Kaiser's son."

"Kaisher wash a papa?"

"Yep. Ba'cho gave him to us."

"Hee'sh going with ush? Hee'sh oursh?"

"That's right."

"Oh, boy! Oh, boy!"

They ride through the town and past Birnbaum's Saloon. Ethan nods at the townsfolk who wave and call out "Good luck" to them. The place appears more vibrant and the people friendlier than when he first arrived and scouted the area. They finally come to the trailhead, and Ethan stops to look up where the high meadows and Morgan ranch are.

"She should have gone with you," Ba'cho comments.

"No," Ethan sighs, "she did the right thing. She followed her heart, and I lost out to somebody better."

"We will watch your trail for many days and make sure no one follows."

"Obliged."